HERMAN
MELVILLE

Moby Dick

白鯨記

Adaptation and Activities by Sara Weiss
Illustrated by Arianna Vairo

The Commercial Press

Contents 目錄

故事錄音開始和結束的標記
start ▶ **stop** ⏹

Ishmael

Ahab

Starbuck

Stubb

Tashtego

Queequeg

Flask

Daggoo

5

Vocabulary

1 **The following adjectives are used to describe either people, places or the weather. Put each word into a group. Some of the adjectives can be used more than once. Use your dictionary to help you.**

> blue • anxious • damp • rainy • sad • cheerful • curious
> wild • disappointed • afraid • astonished

People	Places	Weather
sad		

2 *Moby Dick* **is about the search for a great white whale across the world's seas. Here are some words which you will find in this story. Which of them are used to talk about ships and the sea and which are used to talk about whales and whaling? Use your dictionary to help you.**

> deck • masthead • waves • seasick • drown • mast • harpoon •
> seawater • hull • stern • sink • crow's nest • harpooneer •
> rope • hunt • sail • oil • hump • spout • bow

ships/the sea	whales/whaling
deck	

Writing

3 **Write four sentences using the words from the previous two exercises (and any other necessary words).**

Sailors aren't afraid of feeling seasick because they're used to high waves and rainy weather.

1 ....

2 ....

3 ....

4 ....

Vocabulary

4 **These are words you will find in the first chapter. Match each word to the correct definition. Use your dictionary to help you.**

1 ☐ purse

2 ☐ dismal

3 ☐ ominous

4 ☐ embalmed

5 ☐ tomahawk

6 ☐ to snore

7 ☐ sermon

8 ☐ chaplain

9 ☐ to whittle

10 ☐ to hum

a to sing a tune quietly, with closed lips, not using any words

b a religious leader

c type of tool or weapon similar to a small axe first used by Native Americans

d the noise a person makes every time they breathe when they are sleeping

e sad, gloomy, depressing

f when a dead body is preserved by using chemicals or spices

g suggesting that something bad is going to happen

h to make something from a piece of wood by repeatedly cutting or slicing it

i a talk on a moral or religious subject usually said by a religious person

j small bag made of leather for carrying money

Chapter One

Planning the Voyage

▶ 2 Call me Ishmael. Some years ago – it isn't important exactly when – I had very little money and nothing to do so I decided to sail around the world. Traveling makes me feel healthy. Whenever I feel sad, whenever it feels like a damp, rainy November in my soul, I know it's time to get to sea as soon as possible.

Now, when I say that I am in the habit of going to sea whenever this bad mood occurs, I do not mean to say that I ever go as a passenger. To go as a passenger means you must have a purse, and a purse is no good unless you have something in it. Besides, passengers get seasick. They fight with each other, they don't sleep well at night and do not enjoy themselves very much. No, I never go as a passenger. I always go to sea as a sailor, especially because I am paid for it. Passengers are never paid a single penny that I have ever heard of. Another reason I go to sea as a sailor is for the healthy exercise and the clean air around me.

The most important of my reasons for going to sea however, is the incredible idea of the great whale itself. Such an important and mysterious monster makes me extremely curious. The wild and distant seas where this gigantic creature swims – I am tormented with a constant desire for these far-away places. I love to sail in dangerous seas, and land on wild coasts. For all these reasons, the whaling voyage was very exciting.

I packed a shirt or two, and an extra pair of trousers into my old suitcase and went to New Bedford, in Massachusetts. It was a Saturday night in December when I arrived. I was disappointed at the news that I had missed the last ferry to Nantucket Island, the place where the most important and best whaling ships departed from. Since there would not be another boat to that famous old island until Monday, I had a night, a day and still another night to spend in New Bedford. Finding a place to eat and sleep soon became a serious concern. It was a very dark and dismal night, bitterly cold and cheerless, and I knew no one in the place. With slow steps I walked up and down the streets, looking for accommodation. I passed a few inns that looked too expensive. Then at last I saw a dim light, not far from the docks and, looking up, saw a sign over the door with the name The Spouter-Inn: Peter Coffin. It seemed a rather ominous name to me. "Spouter? Coffin?" Coffins are for dead people, but it's a common name in Nantucket. It seemed an odd sort of place, but it didn't look expensive so I went in.

As I entered, I found a group of young seamen sitting around a table. I looked for the landlord[1] and told him I wanted a room. He told me that his inn was full – there wasn't a bed unoccupied. "But look, if you have no objections to sharing a room with another sailor, you can stay here. If you're going sailing, you'll have to get used to that sort of thing." I told him that I never liked to sleep two in a bed; that if I did, it would depend completely on who the harpooneer might be but if he (the landlord) had no other room for me, and the harpooneer wasn't horrible, I would put up with sharing the room. "I thought so," said the landlord. "All right, take a seat. Supper? – you want supper? Supper will be ready directly."

1. landlord: 房東

After a while, four or five of us men went to supper in the room next door. It was as cold as Iceland – no fire at all – the landlord said he couldn't afford it. We had to button up our jackets and hold cups of boiling tea with our freezing fingers. There was a lot of food though – not only meat and potatoes but dessert too!

It was now about 9.00pm and I wanted to go up to my room. No man likes to sleep two in a bed, and when it comes to sleeping with an unknown stranger, in a strange inn, in a strange town, and that stranger is a harpooneer, then your objections multiply. The more I thought about this harpooneer, the more I hated the idea of sleeping with him. It was fair to presume that being a harpooneer, his clothes would not be the cleanest and certainly not the finest. I began to shake all over. "What kind of man is this?" I asked the landlord. It was now 12 midnight and he hadn't returned. "Generally he's an early bird," said the landlord, "but tonight he went out to sell his head." "Sell his head?" I asked, "Are you telling me this man is actually trying to sell his head around the town?" "That's precisely it," replied the landlord, "but I told him he couldn't sell it here, the market's overstocked." "With what?" I shouted. "With heads to be sure; aren't there too many heads in this world?" the landlord replied. "Landlord," I said, "you must stop teasing me, who and what is this harpooneer?" "Well, this harpooneer has just arrived from the South Seas, from New Zealand where he bought a lot of embalmed, human heads to sell here. He's not a dangerous man," the landlord told me. I was so exhausted that, despite my fears, I decided to go upstairs to my room.

I had just managed to fall asleep when I was awakened by the sound of heavy footsteps entering the room. Lord save me, I thought,

as a tall, dark-skinned man walked into the room, holding a New Zealand head. At first I couldn't see his face, then suddenly he turned round. What a sight, such a face! It was dark purple in color, with some yellow parts, completely covered in tattoos! I had never seen a face like that before. Ignorance is the parent of fear and I was so afraid of him that I didn't have the courage to say anything. He began to get undressed; I saw the same colored tattoos covering his arms and chest. He didn't see me however, and when he got into bed, he suddenly felt me lying there next to him. "Who the devil are you?" he said, "You no speak, I kill you!" He grabbed his tomahawk and began waving it at me. "Landlord, landlord, Peter Coffin, help me!" I screamed as I jumped out of the bed. "Speak-ee, tell-ee me who you are," shouted the cannibal[1], again waving his tomahawk in the air. At that moment, thank God, the landlord came into the room, carrying a light.

"Don't be afraid now," the landlord said with a laugh, "Queequeg won't hurt a hair on your head." "Stop laughing," I yelled, "why didn't you tell me that my room-mate was a cannibal?" "I thought you'd have known, once I told you he was walking around the town, selling heads!" He turned to Queequeg, the cannibal, and said, "Do you understand, this man sleeps with you, understand?" "I understand, plenty," said Queequeg, who was smoking a pipe and sitting in the bed. "You get in," Queequeg said, motioning me to the bed with his tomahawk and throwing his clothes to one side. He did this in a very civil way, he was also really kind and charitable. I looked at him for a moment. For all his tattoos, he was, on the whole, a clean, decent looking cannibal. What's all this fuss I've been making, I thought to myself, the man's a human being just as I am: he has just as much reason to fear me as I have to be afraid of him. Better to sleep with a

1. cannibal: 食人族

sober cannibal than a drunken Christian. I got into bed, turned over and never slept better in my life.

When I woke up in the morning, Queequeg was still sleeping. I felt trapped in the bed – if I moved, he would wake up. I had to get up however, so I tried to shake him. "Queequeg!" but his only response was a snore. I kept calling his name and moving my arms and legs until finally he woke up. He rubbed his eyes and looked at me, as if he didn't completely remember how I came to be there. When at last he understood the situation, he got out of bed quickly and using gestures in a kind of sign language, made me understand that he would dress first and then leave me to dress, in private. He is treating me with great respect, I thought, while I have been rudely staring at him. You don't find a man as polite and respectful as Queequeg every day. I decided this was going to be a very interesting voyage.

Later I decided to take a walk around the town of New Bedford. The night before, seeing a man like Queequeg, with tattoos from head to toe and dressed in strange clothes, had been astonishing, but that was only the beginning of astonishing sights in this seaside city. There were people from all around the world – Mediterranean mariners whistled at frightened ladies, sailors from Malaysia and Bombay walked the streets and actual cannibals stood chatting at street corners. All of this made a stranger like me stare.

But New Bedford isn't just famous for its people. It's famous for whales! Had it not been for whalemen like myself, New Bedford might have been forgotten, but thanks to whale hunting, thanks to the quest for precious whale oil, it was a very important and expensive place to live.

New Bedford also has a chapel – a Whalemen's Chapel. All men who are planning to go whale hunting make a Sunday visit to the chapel. After returning from my morning walk, I again went out, this time to go to a sermon. I saw a small group of sailors, sailors' wives and their widows[1], sitting in the church. The chaplain had not yet arrived but there was silence everywhere. Everyone was waiting for Father Mapple, who had once been a sailor and a harpooneer himself. I sat next to the door and was surprised to see Queequeg near me. The pulpit[2] was the strangest I had ever seen – it was very high like most pulpits, but instead of having a wooden ladder to get to the top, there was one made of rope – just like those you find on a ship! When Father Mapple arrived, he grabbed the rope and climbing hand over hand, went straight up into the pulpit of his 'ship'!

Father Mapple started his sermon, it was all about Jonah and how he was swallowed by a whale. I understood why he was telling us the story, but it frightened me quite a lot.

After the sermon, I returned to the Spouter Inn and found Queequeg there, sitting on a bench by the fire, whittling on his little wooden idol and humming to himself in his devilish way. I sat watching him with much interest. Even though he was a savage, with his face ruined – at least to my taste – by his tattoos, he had an agreeable, friendly appearance. You cannot hide the soul. Despite all his pagan[3] tattoos, I thought I saw the traces of a simple honest heart. He looked courageous and honest. Perhaps it is ridiculous but his face reminded me of George Washington – he was George Washington turned into a cannibal.

I sat down with him and we tried to talk as best we could about all the sights to see in New Bedford. I began to feel the warmth of a

1. **widows:** 寡婦
2. **pulpit:** 講道壇
3. **pagan:** 異教的

new friendship, and even though a man of my closed, reserved world would have thought it too soon to become friends, with this man those old rules did not apply.

Queequeg told me about himself. He was from an island in the South Pacific, an island far away to the West and South. His father was a High Chief, a King, his uncle a High Priest. His mother and his aunts were related to noble warriors, there was royal blood in his veins[1]. He wasn't interested in being a king however – he wanted adventure, he wanted to be a whaler and visit Christian lands. He didn't want to be a Christian though, he had learned they could be just as bad as the people they tried to convert!

1. **veins:** 血管

Reading Comprehension

1 **Answer the following questions about Chapter One.**

1 Who is the narrator of the story?
2 Where is he going?
3 Why does he decide to leave?
4 Who is the cannibal?
5 In what way does the narrator's opinion about Queequeg change?

Word Formation for FIRST

2 **Read the text below. Use the word in capitals at the end of each line to form a word that fits the gap in the same line.**

The whale Moby Dick is not a normal character
because we cannot know its thoughts, feelings
or (**1**) ....   **INTENT**
It is an (**2**) .... force which has been   **PERSONAL**
considered in many different ways by literary
experts. Moby Dick might be a religious symbol
which is all powerful and (**3**) .... or a   **MYSTERY**
metaphor which represents the
(**4**) .... aspects of life. Ishmael   **HIDE**
tells us he cannot see the whale because
it swims under the water. The reader doesn't
know much about Ishmael either. We know he
goes (**5**) .... when he feels sad,   **SAIL**
but we never learn what has caused his
(**6**) .... The story of Moby Dick is   **HAPPY**
very (**7**) .... but not everything   **ROMANCE**
makes (**8**) .... sense.   **LOGIC**

3 Put the correct form of the verb *to choose* or the noun (*choice*) into each sentence.

Ishmael, the narrator of Moby Dick, made an important
(**1**) .... when he decided to go to sea on a whaling ship.
In Chapter one he told us that he (**2**) .... whaling
because he needed to change his life. He could have
(**3**) .... something else such as becoming a soldier, but
instead he (**4**) .... a very dangerous job as a sailor.
What would you have (**5**) .... if you had been Ishmael?
The (**6**) .... of whaling means Ishmael will travel all
around the world, but he won't be comfortable and he could be
in danger. If he had (**7**) .... to be a soldier, he wouldn't
have been any safer.

4 Countable or uncountable nouns. Underline the correct option.

1 Can you please give me some *informations / information?*
2 Ishmael hasn't got any *luggage / luggages.*
3 The whalers went on some *tour / tours* in the South Pacific.
4 Starbuck gives Ishmael *an / some* advice about whaling.
5 Luckily they heard *a / some* news about the bad weather
before sailing into the storm.

PRE-READING ACTIVITY

Vocabulary

5 Match the correct word from the list on the left to the definition.

1 ☐ *Ahoy There!*
2 ☐ To hire
3 ☐ Mercy
4 ☐ Prophecy

a A statement that tells what will happen in the future.

b A kind or forgiving attitude towards a person who has done something bad.

c To employ someone for a job or period of time.

d A phrase used by sailors to get the attention of other sailors.

Chapter Two

The Whaling Ship

The next day we decided to take a boat to Nantucket Port to look for work on a whaling ship. It was very important to choose the right ship because we would be living on it, at sea, for the next three years. As we traveled closer to the port, I realized with great surprise that Queequeg wanted me to decide which ship to choose. He told me he had been talking to his little wooden idol about how to choose the ship. Queequeg thought his idol was a god. The idol insisted that I make the choice. I did not like this plan at all. Queequeg had more experience on ships than I did so I was happy to trust in his judgment. He didn't want to listen to my protests however; I understood it was my responsibility to choose.

When I got to the port, I walked around looking at all the ships and people and, after questioning some men, I learned that there were three ships which were offering voyages of three years. The *Devil-Dam,* the *Tit-bit* and the *Pequod*. The Pequod was named after an old tribe of Native Americans from Massachusetts, so I chose that ship. It seemed perfect for us. It had an elegance, a kind of noble but sad quality that I liked. I began looking around the deck of the Pequod for someone in authority in order to sign up as a sailor. At first I saw nobody, but I couldn't help seeing a strange little structure

that looked like a tent, in the middle of the deck. When I looked more closely I saw a man inside this tent, a man with a very brown, sunburnt face, like most seamen. "Ahoy," I said, "Are you the captain of this ship?" "No!" replied the man, "I hire the crew for this ship. My name's Peleg. What do you want?"

"My friend and I want to sign up for the voyage." "Have you ever been on a whaling ship before?" asked Peleg. "No sir, I never have." "So you don't know anything about whaling, do you?" "Nothing sir, but I have no doubt I'll learn soon. I've been on several sailing voyages." "Sailing, that's different! Why do you want to go whaling?" "I want to see what whaling is, I want to see the world." "You want to see what whaling is, do you? Have you met Captain Ahab yet? Ahab is the captain of this ship, he's the one-legged captain. He's famous to all sailors!" Peleg exclaimed. "What do you mean, sir?" I asked, "Was the other one lost to a whale?" "Lost to a whale! It was chewed, chopped and eaten by the biggest, most dangerous whale that ever came near a boat! Young man, are you still sure you want to go on a three year whaling journey? Are you brave enough? Can you use a harpoon, even when you are attacked by a huge monster whale?" "I can, sir." "Ok, you'll do very well."

With his harpoon in hand, Queequeg arrived to sign up for the voyage. As soon as Captain Peleg saw him he shouted, "I don't let any cannibals on my ship! Unless they can show me their legal papers!" "What do you mean by that Captain Peleg?" I said. "I mean, he must show his papers. He must prove he's part of a Christian church. Are you in communion with any Christian church?" "He's a member of the First Congregational Church," I said. "How long has he been a member?" the captain asked, "Young man, you're not telling me the

truth." "Queequeg is just as Christian as you and I, as all good people are. We are all God's children, aren't we?" I insisted. "Young man, you'd be a better missionary[1] than a whaler. All right, come aboard, he can sign up," said Peleg.

So we went down into the cabin where, to my great joy, Queequeg soon became part of the whaling ship's crew, officially.

Queequeg and I had just left the Pequod and were walking along the water when we heard a strange voice. "Shipmates, have you signed up for that ship?" A crazy, badly dressed man was pointing at the Pequod as he spoke to us. "You mean the Pequod?" I said. "Yes, the Pequod, that ship there," he said. "Yes, we have just signed up," I replied. "But that ship is destined to die, to sink in the dark black sea!" "Die, sink, what are you talking about?" I shouted. "Who are you to say such things to us?" "I'm Elijah," he said. He looked at us with madness in his eyes and said, "God have mercy on your souls." "Queequeg, let's go," I said, "This man is crazy." "You haven't met Captain Ahab yet, have you?" said Elijah. "What do you know about Captain Ahab?" I asked. "What's done is done, there's no turning back now," said Elijah as he walked away from us. 'Elijah', the name of a prophet, I said to myself. But this man is not important, he doesn't know what he's talking about. It's all nonsense. I was preparing for a fantastic sea adventure and the crazy words of a total stranger were not going to destroy my plans.

Now I was really curious to meet Captain Ahab, the infamous whale hunter with only one leg.

There was a lot to do before I met him. The Pequod was preparing for a three year journey, and we had to do a lot of work before our departure day, the 25th of December, Christmas!

---

1. **missionary:** 傳教士

A ship like the Pequod was too expensive to have just one owner. A group of people, often an entire town, all owned a part of the ship. Retired sailors, shopkeepers, teachers, widows and widowers[1] each paid for a small part of the ship. That's why it was so important for the Pequod to be successful in her hunt for whales – all the owners depended on the money they would earn from the Pequod's whales. Queequeg and I spent a lot of time on the ship, helping in the preparations, but we never once saw Captain Ahab.

We met the other members of the crew, however. Starbuck was the Chief or First Mate of the Pequod. He was a native of Nantucket, a Quaker, and although he was only 30 years old, his years at sea made him seem older. He was a brave, honest man with pure, tight skin and a thin, fit body. He was good looking and you could see his inner vitality when you looked into his eyes. He didn't talk much but respected the men who worked for him on the ship. "I will have no man in my boat who is not afraid of whales." This was Starbuck's belief. He believed a man had to understand the enormous danger he faced to be a good whale hunter. Stubb, the ship's Second Mate, told us, "Starbuck, he is as careful a man as you'll find anywhere in whale hunting." Stubb was a practical man from the town Cape Cod. Stubb thought courage was a useful instrument and nothing more. In the business of whaling, courage was a very important necessity on the ship, and shouldn't be wasted foolishly. The Third Mate was named Flask and came from Martha's Vineyard. He was a short, sturdy man who believed he had a duty to hunt whales. He seemed to be angry at whales, as if the entire breed of animals had somehow offended him.

These three mates – Starbuck, Stubb and Flask – were important men. If we think of Captain Ahab as a general, these men were his

1. **widowers:** 鰥夫

majors. They commanded the Pequod's fishing boats which were used, once a whale had been found, to take the sailors directly on the hunt. Each of these men had his own soldier, or harpooneer, who were experts at attacking whales. Starbuck chose Queequeg as his personal harpooneer. Stubb, the Second Mate, chose a Native American named Tashtego, to be his harpooneer. Tashtego was from Martha's Vineyard and was known for his great skill at whale hunting. The third harpooneer was Daggoo, a tall, strong man from Africa, who had been chosen by Third Mate Flask. The men laughed quietly whenever they saw Daggoo and Flask together; Daggoo seemed like a tall, elegant giraffe when he stood next to short, square Flask!

The other sailors in the crew came from all around the world. They came from Wales, Greenland, the Azores and the Shetland Islands. Everyone knows that islanders make the best seamen. The crew of an American whaling ship is like the American military; its officers are all American born, but its sailors are almost never *born* in the United States, they *become* American citizens after coming from somewhere else.

We left Nantucket on Christmas Day but I still hadn't seen Captain Ahab, even a few days after our departure. The three Mates gave the orders, but they were the only people who went down into the cabin to meet with our mysterious captain. They seemed to be the only commanders of the ship. Yes, the supreme lord and dictator was there, somewhere on the ship, but none of the common seamen like me had been permitted to see him.

Every time I came onto the deck, I looked up to where the captain would be, but never saw him. While I had first felt a normal curiosity about Ahab, I now felt more and more nervous about our unknown captain. My nervousness increased when I remembered Elijah's crazy words, even though I tried to forget his frightening prophecy. Luckily, the attitude of the three chief officers, the Mates, helped me to feel cheerful and optimistic about our voyage.

When we left Nantucket, the weather had been polar cold, but as we travelled to southern seas, the temperatures grew warmer and it was more pleasant to stand on the deck and enjoy the ocean breezes. It was on a warm, cloudy morning when I finally saw Captain Ahab on the quarterdeck[1].

1. quarterdeck: 後甲板

Stop & Check

1 **Are these sentences about Chapter Two true (T) or false (F)?**
If there isn't enough information, choose doesn't say (DS).

T F DS

1 Queequeg wanted Ishmael to choose the whaling
ship Devil-Dam. ☐ ☐ ☐

2 The Pequod was named for an old tribe of Native
Americans from Montana. ☐ ☐ ☐

3 Peleg is not the captain of the Pequod. ☐ ☐ ☐

4 Ishamel has no experience on whaling ships. ☐ ☐ ☐

5 Peleg thinks Ishmael is probably a brave
young man. ☐ ☐ ☐

6 Queequeg has papers to prove he is part of the
Congregational Church. ☐ ☐ ☐

7 Elijah is a sailor. ☐ ☐ ☐

8 Elijah predicts disaster for the Pequod's voyage. ☐ ☐ ☐

9 The Pequod is owned by one very rich man. ☐ ☐ ☐

10 Mr. Starbuck is the captain of the Pequod. ☐ ☐ ☐

11 All of the sailors on the Pequod come from the
United States. ☐ ☐ ☐

12 Ishmael has met Captain Ahab. ☐ ☐ ☐

Writing

2 **Imagine you are Ishmael. Write a letter to a friend, telling him/**
her about your arrival in Nantucket Port, the ship, its crew and
your feelings about the voyage.

....

....

....

....

First – Gapfill

3 **Read the summary of Chapters One and Two and put in a word that makes the most sense. The first one is done as an example.**

The story of Moby Dick begins with an ...*introduction*... that has become famous (**1**) .... the literary world: "Call me Ishmael". Ishmael is an unhappy young man who wants adventure. We are in New York city but (**2**) .... travel with Ishmael to New Bedford, Massachusetts which is the whaling capital of the U.S. Ishmael (**3**) .... why he wants to be a sailor, and not just a normal passenger – he doesn't have the money to (**4**) .... for a ticket.

(**5**) .... he arrives in New Bedford, Ishmael meets Queequeg. They become friends very quickly and decide to (**6**) .... the crew of the whaling ship Pequod. They meet a strange man named Elijah (**7**) .... frightens Ishmael but (**8**) .... their voyage begins he forgets his fear and is very thrilled to be at sea.

PRE-READING ACTIVITIES

Vocabulary

4 **Match the correct word from the list on the left to a definition on the right.**

1 ☐ peg leg
2 ☐ hint
3 ☐ evidence
4 ☐ stroll
5 ☐ perdition
6 ☐ lance

a a slow, relaxed walk
b a punishment after death, which lasts forever
c a weapon with a long, wooden handle and a sharp, pointed metal head
d a false leg, made of wood or ivory, to replace a human leg
e a small sign or indication given to someone by something
f information that gives a strong reason for believing something

5 The following sentences are all part of a conversation between Captain Ahab and First Mate Starbuck. Put the sentences in order. The first one (1) has been done for you.

☐ 7 Captain Ahab: "Mr. Starbuck, will you help me find Moby Dick, my enemy?"

☐ Starbuck: "The whale attacked you because it's an animal; that's what animals do, but you hunt him for revenge and that's crazy!"

☐ Captain Ahab: "But do you promise? Will you hunt Moby Dick across the seas without giving up?"

☐ Starbuck: "I am here to hunt whales, I will help you captain."

☐ Captain Ahab: "I will be rich when I have killed the great white whale. That is my revenge."

☐ Starbuck: "I'm a whaler, I don't give up easily! I hunt whales because I want to earn a lot of money."

☐ Captain Ahab: "Money? You only care about money! Moby Dick took my leg. I will take the whale's life, I don't care about getting rich!"

Grammar for First and Listening

▶ 4 **6** Read the text below and choose the best option (A, B, C, D) for each gap. Then listen to the first part of the next chapter to check your answers.

He looked (**1**) .... a Renaissance statue of a Greek god – tall, strong and solid. His face was marked by a long, thin scar that went from his forehead to his cheek and down his neck. I asked (**2**) .... how far it went. Whether he was born that way, or (**3**) .... it was a scar left by a horrible accident, no one could say with certainty. Nobody in the crew ever said (**4**) .... about it, but some sailors believed Ahab had gotten the scar during a (**5**) .... with a whale.

1 **A** to	**B** to	**C** at	**D** like
2 **A** myself	**B** himself	**C** itself	**D** me
3 **A** weather	**B** as	**C** whether	**D** when
4 **A** something	**B** nothing	**C** anything	**D** anyone
5 **A** violence	**B** fight	**C** argue	**D** attack

Chapter Three

Captain Ahab and his Quest

▶ 3   He looked like a Renaissance statue of a Greek god – tall, strong and solid. His face was marked by a long, thin scar that went from his forehead to his cheek and down his neck. I asked myself how far it went. Whether he was born that way, or whether it was a scar left by a horrible accident, no one could say with certainty. Nobody in the crew ever said anything about it, but some sailors believed Ahab had gotten the scar during a fight with a whale. ■

▶ 4   I was so powerfully affected by his grim appearance that it took some time for me to realize I hadn't even noticed his white peg leg. It had been made from the bone of a sperm whale by the ship's carpenter[1]. Ahab placed his peg leg in a specially made hole on the quarterdeck so he could find his balance despite the rocking movement caused by the ocean's waves. It didn't look particularly comfortable, and when he stood on it, you could see by his face he felt great pain. I was impressed by how tall and straight he stood, looking out over the ocean. He didn't say a word and no one spoke to him. It was clear that his officers were very aware of his presence; their gestures and expressions showed how uncomfortable they felt as their silent, unhappy master watched over them from above. ■

1. carpenter: 木匠

5   That morning, after only a few minutes on the deck, he returned to his cabin. As the days continued however and the temperatures grew warmer, he was seen every day by the crew. He would stand with his leg in its special little hole or sit on an ivory stool or walk slowly up and down the deck of the ship. He seemed as unnecessary as another mast, because the Pequod was only making a quiet, slow passage now, we were not hunting.

The three Mates were responsible for supervising the day to day activities so there was little or nothing for Ahab to do. The warmer weather and calm sea seemed gradually to change his mood; it was actually possible to see a small smile on his long, thin face.

It was during the more pleasant weather that I had my turn at the masthead. 'Manning[1] the masthead' was a job that all of us seamen had to do. There was a regular rotation and each man had to take his turn. Manning the masthead is an ancient and interesting job. A sailor has to stand on a small platform, which is attached to the masthead in the middle of the ship, high above the deck. The sailor has one responsibility – look for whales! When you stand at that height, you can see for miles. Seeing or 'sighting' whales was the most important job on the ship. It seems the Egyptians were the first to stand in mastheads and there's no evidence of anyone doing it before them. Manning the masthead is not an easy job. Not all whaling ships have what are called 'crow's nests' in which the sailor standing in the masthead is protected from bad weather and freezing temperatures. Luckily for us, the Pequod was sailing in southern seas, so it was often very comfortable to be a 'mastheadman', relaxing high up in the sky, as the waves gently rocked the ship. I confess I was probably not the best sailor for the job! How many whales escaped capture when I was

1. **manning:** 操控，控制

manning the mast I'll never know. I was too busy day-dreaming to watch for them.

The weather grew warmer and life on the ship was tranquil[1]. One morning shortly after breakfast, Captain Ahab took his usual walk along the deck. Most sea captains usually walk at that hour, just like country gentlemen who go for a stroll around their gardens.

Soon we could hear his distinct yet strange walk - one normal step, one with the sound of his ivory leg hitting the ship's wooden deck. If you looked at his face, you could see something strange there as well. The wrinkles on his forehead, those deep lines we were used to seeing, seemed deeper than ever before, as if he had had a very bad night, without any sleep, tortured by nightmares and memories. "Do you see him, Flask?" whispered Stubb, "his thoughts are going to burst out of his head, there'll be an explosion soon."

The hours passed as Ahab walked up and down the deck. He returned to his cabin, then he left his cabin, again and again, with an intense, dark expression on his face. It was almost the end of the day when he suddenly stopped, right at the place on the deck where he could put his peg leg into its pivot hole. He was able to keep his balance by holding a sail with one hand. Then he ordered Starbuck to call all the sailors to the deck. "Yes Sir!" said Starbuck, who was astonished at the order; such a command was almost never given on a ship, except in an extraordinary case or an emergency.

"Send everybody to the front. Mastheadmen, come down!" repeated Ahab. When everyone was assembled, looking at him with curious and anxious faces, for he looked a lot like the horizon when a storm is approaching, Ahab began to walk back and forth in front of the men. He had his head bent down as if he didn't notice the

---

1. tranquil: 寧靜的

men, who were whispering nervously to each other. Captain Ahab was very frightening.

"What do you do when you see a whale, men?" cried Captain Ahab.

"Call out for him!" said the men, in unison.

"Good!" said Ahab, with strong approval in his voice. He could see the enthusiasm in his men. "And what do you do next, men?"

"Lower the fishing boats and begin the hunt!"

"That's right," shouted Ahab. The old captain seemed happier and happier, his face full of joyful approval. At that moment, Captain Ahab turned around in his pivot hole and reached up to grab onto another sail. "Do you see this men, do you see this ounce of Spanish gold?" he said, holding up a large, bright coin in the sun. "Look at this, it's a sixteen dollar piece, men. Do you see it? Mr. Starbuck, help me, give me a hammer." Receiving the hammer from the First Mate, the captain walked forward to the main-mast holding the hammer up high in the air, with one hand. His other hand held the gold coin, and in a loud voice he shouted, "Whoever sees a white whale with a damaged brow[1] and a crooked jaw[2]; whoever sees a white whale with three holes in his side; whoever sees this particular whale shall have this ounce of gold!" Then he nailed the coin onto the masthead.

"Hooray! Hooray!" shouted the men.

"Listen to me men, listen to me! This is not an ordinary whale, it's got a harpoon in its hump – that's my harpoon – it's Moby Dick that's got my harpoon – I put it there myself!"

"Captain Ahab," said Starbuck, "I have heard of Moby Dick – but wasn't it Moby Dick who took off your leg?"

"Who told you that?" cried Ahab, "Yes Starbuck, it was Moby Dick, he did this to me. Yes, yes, Moby Dick did this cruel thing to me."

---

1. **brow:** 前額   2. **jaw:** 下顎

Ahab cried out, with a horrible sound like an animal, "I'll chase him around the Cape of Good Hope, around the Horn of Africa, all the way to the flames of perdition before I give up. What do you say men, are you with me, will you help me?"

"Yes, Yes!" shouted the seamen and harpooneers, running up close to their captain. "A sharp eye to see a white whale, a sharp knife for Moby Dick!"

"God bless you men," Ahab said, with a desperate voice. "God bless you men. Starbuck, are you with me too, will you chase Moby Dick with me?"

"I am here to chase whales, and I will hunt Moby Dick, but not for my captain's personal revenge," said Starbuck. "I hunt whales for business. How many barrels of precious whale oil can we have with revenge? Revenge will not bring much money at the Nantucket market!"

"Money," shouted Ahab, "is that all that's important to you? Revenge will make me a rich man, here, inside me," cried Ahab, beating his chest with his hand.

"That whale attacked your boat, and you, because *you* attacked *him*. That is what wild animals do, that's their instinct. You hunt him out of cruelty and revenge, that's crazy!" insisted Starbuck.

"Crazy? You say I am crazy? Listen to me Starbuck! Moby Dick is not just a stupid animal, he is bad, he is evil. That is what I hate, his evilness!" Starbuck turned and as he was walking away, he whispered to himself, "God protect us all, protect us all" with a sad, troubled face. Captain Ahab was so lost in his own thoughts he didn't hear what the First Mate said.

"Bring me a cup, bring me a cup!" shouted Ahab. Holding the cup in his hand, Ahab turned to the harpooneers and ordered them to

show their weapons. He arranged the men in a line, all with their harpoons in their hands, while his three Mates stood at his side with their lances. The rest of the seamen formed a circle around the group. Ahab stood silently for a moment, staring at each man in the eyes – eyes that seemed like a wolf's eyes staring back at their leader. "Drink from the cup and pass," he shouted as he gave the cup, which was filled with wine, to the closest harpooneer. "Drink, drink! We are united!" he cried, "Mates, mates, come forward, forward, hold your weapons up, everyone in a circle!" First he looked at Starbuck, then at Stubb, then at Flask. From Starbuck, to Stubb, to Flask. "Now, swear this: death to Moby Dick. God punish us all if we don't punish Moby Dick!" The three Mates shook with fear, was their captain crazy? Stubb and Flask looked from side to side; the honest eyes of Starbuck stared down at his feet. Ahab faced the three harpooneers and said, "Now you three, drink to the death of Moby Dick." As Ahab walked slowly towards his cabin he stopped, turned to the men and said, "Remember this well. You have all made a promise. You have promised to kill Moby Dick."

I, Ishmael was one of those men. I had shouted along with them, I had promised to kill Moby Dick. Captain Ahab's obsession with the great white whale had become my obsession. I listened carefully to the story of that murderous animal that we seamen had promised to kill. Starbuck said that whales do what they do because of instinct, nothing more. What I had just heard about this white whale was very different.

FIRST - Listening

▶ 4 **1 Can you remember the words to complete this passage from Chapter Three? Listen and check.**

> spoke • impressed • unhappy • bone • rocking movement •
> gestures • quarterdeck • appearance

I was so powerfully affected by his grim (**1**) .... that
it took some time for me to realize I hadn't even noticed his
white peg leg. It had been made from the (**2**) .... of a
Sperm whale by the ship's carpenter. Ahab placed his peg leg
in a specially made hole on the (**3**) .... so he could find
his balance despite the (**4**) .... caused by the ocean's
waves. It didn't look particularly comfortable, and when he stood
on it, you could see by his face he felt great pain. I was
(**5**) .... by how tall and straight he stood, looking out
over the ocean. He didn't say a word and no one (**6**) ....
to him. You could tell his officers were very aware of his
presence; their (**7**) .... and expressions showed how
uncomfortable they felt as their silent, (**8**) .... master
watched over them from above.

Writing

**2 What is your opinion of Captain Ahab? Write a short paragraph
describing his appearance, character and say what you think of
him and his actions so far.**

....

....

....

....

3 **Complete the second sentence so that it is very similar to the first sentence, using the word given. Do not change the word given. Use from two to five words to complete the sentences including the word given.**

Example:

The seamen didn't have to do anything when the sea was calm.

nothing

There ....*was nothing*.... the seamen had to do when the sea was calm.

1 It had been made from the bone of a sperm whale by the ship's carpenter.

made

The ship's carpenter .... the bone of a sperm whale.

2 Ahab would walk slowly up and down the deck of the ship.

used

Ahab .... slowly up and down the ship's deck.

3 Manning the masthead is not an easy job.

difficult

.... to man the masthead.

4 Starbuck was so surprised by Ahab's command that he didn't believe it was real.

such

It was .... command from Ahab that Starbuck didn't believe it was real.

5 Starbuck said that he thought Ahab was crazy.

accused

Starbuck .... crazy.

6 Ahab and Ishmael both had the same obsession now.

obsessed

Ahab and Ishmael .... the same thing now.

Vocabulary

4 **Match each word to the correct definition.**

1	☐ haunt		**a**	go down below the surface of water towards
2	☐ likely			the bottom
3	☐ mystical		**b**	to bring in or take out something illegally
4	☐ wrinkled			from one place to another
5	☐ glide		**c**	deliberate punishment or injury in return for
6	☐ chart			what one has suffered
7	☐ revenge		**d**	having a hidden meaning or spiritual power
8	☐ smuggle		**e**	probable or expected
9	☐ sink		**f**	having or showing a small fold, or line in the skin
			g	to move along smoothly and continuously in
				a specific direction
			h	to visit a place regularly (ghosts)
			i	a kind of map of the sea

Prepositions + *ing*

5 **We use the *-ing* form of a verb after a preposition. Complete the following sentences with the correct form of these verbs.**

see • attack • do • go • watch • sleep

Captains and seamen were sometimes able to tell each other about ...*seeing*.... whales.

1 Ishmael had to get used to .... with another person in the same bed.

2 A few captains of whaling ships told stories of .... Moby Dick.

3 Most whale hunters wouldn't dream of .... battle with a Sperm whale.

4 Some seamen didn't understand the risk they took in .... after Moby Dick.

5 Ishmael didn't think he was very good at .... for whales.

Chapter Four

Whales

The story went like this: in the recent past, but only from time to time, the great white whale, who always swam alone, had been in the seas where fishermen most often hunted. Not all the fishermen knew who he was, and only some of them had seen him. Only a few of these whale hunters had actually attacked the famous white whale. There were a lot of whale hunting ships, but since the area they fished in was gigantic, it was normal for whaling boats not to see other ships for quite a long time. Twelve months could pass before a ship saw another ship and the captains and crews were able to talk to each other about Moby Dick. It was likely that some of these ships saw the gigantic, deadly white whale, but given his speed and size, it was also probable the whaling ships had never gotten very close. At this time, captains told stories of attacking a ferocious, fearless whale who attacked the whaling boats and killed the hunters! The great whale Moby Dick became a terrible legend in the southern seas.

Sperm whales in general were always known as the most dangerous in the Leviathan family. There are whale hunters who are happy to hunt the smaller *Greenland* or *Right* whale, but would never dream of doing battle with a Sperm whale. According to zoologists, the Sperm whale is feared by all other creatures in the sea, including

sharks. However, no one knows why the Sperm whale seems to hate the human species.

There was a small number of fishermen who were brave enough to hunt Moby Dick, even though they knew how dangerous their mission would be. There was also a large group of men who didn't really understand the risk they took in going after this white whale but were happy to be part of an exciting, challenging adventure.

Moby Dick had a reputation that seemed almost mystical, and was not always based on reality. He did have very real, physical characteristics however, that were clearly visible and extremely terrifying. It wasn't only his enormous size that made him different from other Sperm whales. He had a strange, snow-white forehead and a tall hump that was shaped like a pyramid. The rest of his body was lined and spotted with a strange, whitish color. He could be seen gliding through the water, leaving milky waves of creamy foam, sparkling under the sun. His injured lower jaw and huge dimensions created terror in everyone who saw him, and so did his incredible wildness – he hunted everyone who hunted him. Many whaling ships were destroyed by Moby Dick, and many whalers had lost arms, legs, even their lives, to his enormous teeth.

The story of one whaling ship that lost the battle against Moby Dick went like this: the whalers in their three small fishing boats surrounded the great white whale. The captain was in the front of one boat, with his harpoon in his hand, ready to attack the whale. That captain was Ahab. All of a sudden Moby Dick's huge head emerged from the water and closed on Ahab's leg, like a giant mower[1] on a field of grass. Somehow Ahab survived. It isn't surprising however, that ever since that almost fatal episode, Ahab had desperately wanted

1. mower: 割草機

revenge against the whale. The great white whale became a symbol for Ahab, he represented all Ahab's anger and frustration in life. He had to kill Moby Dick to find spiritual peace and tranquility. His quest to hunt Moby Dick began then.

If you had followed Captain Ahab down into his cabin that day after his seamen had enthusiastically agreed to join his battle against Moby Dick, you would have seen him analyzing maps of the sea. These sea charts were old, the paper was yellow. He studied the charts intensely and, with a pencil, slowly drew lines on the map. The heavy lamp was rocking from side to side with every movement of the ship, but Ahab was too lost in concentration to notice. He studied his charts night after night, trying to find the best way to catch Moby Dick. It isn't difficult to find Sperm whales, because they swim in charted waters; in fact they are known to be very dependable, always choosing the same 'veins' as they are called. These veins are like invisible roads on the ocean floor. Sperm whales seem guided by a kind of perfect instinct – they always arrive at their chosen destination.

Thanks to Captain Ahab's calculations, the Pequod was sailing in the right direction to find the white whale. Was it possible, though, for a single whaling ship in the middle of a huge ocean to see a particular whale? Ahab was convinced it was. He was obsessed with[1] finding Moby Dick. Nothing would stop him.

Whale hunting is not, in any way, easy. I, Ishmael, have personally known of whales who managed to escape their hunters even after being attacked by harpooneers. They swim away, with the harpoons stuck in their bodies! Certain whales become famous in certain areas; these whales have strange, recognizable marks on their foreheads

1. obsessed with: 着迷

or humps. Some captains of whaling ships have become famous for their bravery in battle, but few have ever caught and killed a sperm whale. Many ships have been destroyed, many sailors have died and many sperm whales have gotten away.

Captain Ahab wanted nothing more than to kill Moby Dick. To reach his goal, Ahab had to use tools and the most useful tools he had were his men. Ahab knew that his First Mate, Starbuck, was a valuable tool. He knew Starbuck was essential in reaching his objective. Ahab also understood that Starbuck did not agree with his desire for revenge. Starbuck hunted Sperm whales so he could sell their oil. Ahab knew that, in difficult situations, men needed to stay calm; they needed to think positively. Ahab knew that he, and the Pequod, had other responsibilities that were not only his personal revenge. As Captain of the ship, he had to hunt all whales in order to get precious sperm whale oil – that should be the main purpose of his journey.

It was a cloudy, humid afternoon and the seamen were lazily lying on the deck, or staring vacantly out at the sea. Queequeg and I were working together, weaving[1] a mat. There was a dreamy quality to the day; the sea was calm and there wasn't much wind at all. Suddenly we heard Tashtego's cry "There she blows! There she blows!" from high up on the masthead. We all looked out to sea and saw a group of Sperm whales who were blowing air and water from the spouts on their backs. The Sperm whale blows like a clock – always the same, always regular. That's how a whaleman can tell it's a Sperm whale and not a smaller whale. This was the first time I'd seen a whale. I'd been waiting weeks for this moment. My heart was beating hard in my chest – I almost couldn't breathe. Was Moby Dick one of the whales we saw? That was impossible, wasn't

1. weaving : 編織

it? Moby Dick always swam alone. The small fishing boats were lowered from the sides of the Pequod and the hunting adventure began. Suddenly, five dark shapes, like phantoms, appeared on the deck, standing in circle around Captain Ahab. Who were these men? These strangers were lowering a harpoon boat on the other side of the ship. At that moment I thought of Elijah, the crazy man I had met before the voyage. Was his prediction of tragedy becoming real? The oldest man in the group was their leader. He was wearing an old jacket of black cotton and black trousers and he had a large, white Turban[1] which was made from his own hair on his head. Ahab shouted out to the old man, "Are you all ready, Fedallah?" "Ready," said the man. "Lower the boats, lower the boats!" commanded Ahab. His voice was so loud and so powerful that the men did what he asked, even though they were shocked by the strangers on the ship.

We were more surprised when we saw, a few moments later, Captain Ahab standing at the front of the boat with the strangers. Ahab was shouting at Starbuck, Stubb and Flask to move the fishing boats away from each other to cover as much space in the water as possible. "Captain Ahab?" said Starbuck. "Spread out, move out!" cried Ahab.

Later I learned that Fedellah was Persian and was Captain Ahab's personal harpooneer. At that moment however I felt very afraid and confused. I had never been in a fishing boat before. I was at eye level with the water and I couldn't see anything because there was so much fog and mist.

Starbuck was the captain of my boat and he was busy following Ahab's orders to follow Stubb's boat. "Mr. Starbuck, please, can I ask you a question?" shouted Stubb. "Hello Stubb, yes, what do you

---

1. Turban: 穆斯林頭巾

want?" was the answer. "What do you think of those strangers, who are they?" "Probably smuggled on board, at night, when we didn't notice. A sad business Mr. Stubb. But never mind Mr. Stubb, all for the best. This is our job – hunting whales!" said Starbuck.

It started to rain as the three boats moved forward. Starbuck, Stubb and Flask urged[1] their men to row faster and faster. I was rowing as fast as my arms would let me, which didn't feel very fast at all. The muscles in my arms and shoulders were hurting. We were competing with each other to be the first boat to reach the whales, but Captain Ahab and his strange whalemen were far ahead of us. "Row, row my boys!" Starbuck told us, not in a loud voice, but in an intense, emotional whisper. We concentrated on rowing fast, we wanted to get to the whales. Suddenly a gigantic Sperm whale came to the surface, right next to our boat! Queequeg threw his harpoon at the whale but he missed. The rain started coming down harder and we couldn't see anything. The whale disappeared under the water. Then, without warning, our boat was lifted out of the water and thrown back against the waves, crashing against the water. Only a miracle saved us from drowning at that point because our boat was full of water. The fog was so thick we couldn't see anything; we couldn't see the other fishing boats and we had no idea where the Pequod was. We managed to pick up our oars[2] and realized the boat wasn't going to sink. The wind got stronger while the waves rocked our boat violently. Suddenly Queequeg stood up with a hand to his ear. Then we could all hear the Pequod coming towards us; it was going to crash into us! We all jumped into the water and the Pequod sailed over our fishing boat – where we had been sitting two minutes earlier! We swam as fast as possible, afraid we'd sink to the bottom of the sea. Then, one by one, we were pulled out of the water and onto the Pequod.

1. **urged:** 催促、力勸 ▶SYN◀ to persuade
2. **oars:** 槳

Comprehension Check

1 **Answer the following questions about Chapter Four.**

1 Why are Sperm whales more dangerous than other kinds of whales?

2 What characteristics distinguished Moby Dick from other Sperm whales?

3 Why does Captain Ahab want revenge?

4 Why does Starbuck hunt white whales?

5 Who is Fedellah?

6 What was the weather like when Ishmael went on his first whale hunt?

7 Describe the accident between the Pequod and Starbuck's fishing boat.

Matching

2 **Match the first part of each sentence to the second part.**

1 ☐ Not all of the fisherman knew who he was,

2 ☐ No one knows why Sperm whales seem

3 ☐ If you had followed Ahab down into his cabin that day,

4 ☐ Many ships have been destroyed, many sailors have died

5 ☐ There was a dreamy quality to the day;

a the sea was calm and there wasn't much wind at all.

b and only some of the men had seen him.

c and many sperm whales have gotten away.

d to hate the human species more than any other.

e you would have seen him analyzing maps of the sea.

Vocabulary

3 **Complete the following definitions with the correct word from the box.**

> teasing • soaking wet • capsizing • will and testament •
> joke • kneel • argue • jet • condemned • torment

1 If you are .... to do something, you have no choice; you have to do it.

2 When the seamen get on their knees to wash the deck, they ....

3 The moment a ship is turning over it is ....

4 A source of pain or anxiety is a ....

5 When someone tries to provoke you in a playful or unkind way they are .... you.

6 A strong, narrow stream of liquid or air which is forced out of a small opening is a ....

7 Ishmael was .... after he fell from the fishing boat into the sea.

8 If you believe strongly in something, you .... to defend your idea.

9 A legal document in which someone explains to whom they want to give their property and money after their death is a ....

10 A situation or something someone says that makes you laugh is a ....

4 Complete the sentences with the expressions in the box.

> ~~catch his breath~~ • catch on • catch hold of •
> take seriously • take sides • take a break

After Ishmael was pulled out of the water, he tried to
catch his breath .

1 It is better not to .... some things in life too
....

2 The seamen on the Pequod never had much time to
....

3 It was easy for Queequeg to .... to what
Ishmael said even though he didn't speak English perfectly.

4 When seamen .... against their captain it is
called a mutiny.

5 Ishmael tried to .... the fishing boat but it was
impossible and he fell into the sea.

Prediction

5 **Look at the illustration on page 53. Ishmael and Stubb are talking. What do you think they are talking about? Discuss with a partner.**

Writing

6 **Look again at the illustration on page 53.**
Describe Ishmael and Stubb (how they look, their clothing, their feelings...)

Ishmael ....
....
....

Stubb ....
....
....

Chapter Five

The Voyage Continues

▶ 6   There are certain unusual times in life when what you are doing, the situations you find yourself in, all seem like an enormous joke. You cannot take what happens around you seriously because if you do, the seriousness of everything might be too difficult to tolerate[1]. When you are feeling this way, the universe seems surprisingly cheerful; all difficulties and worries, even danger, seem distant and improbable[2] – someone out there is teasing you, nothing bad can possibly happen to you.

Well, there is nothing like the dangers of whaling to make sailors think like this. After the first battle with a whale, I started thinking just this way. When they pulled me out of the water, the last man to be saved from the sea, I lay on the deck, trying to catch my breath. Shaking my jacket to throw off the water, I asked Queequeg, "Queequeg my friend, does this sort of thing happen often?" Without much emotion, though soaking wet and breathing hard just like me, he told me that such things did happen while whaling, very often. "Mr. Stubb," I asked the Second Mate, who was now calmly smoking his pipe in the rain, "Mr. Stubb, did you not tell us that Mr. Starbuck was one of the most cautious, calmest chief mates you'd ever met? I imagine then that for you, being attacked

1. tolerate: 容忍   2. improbable: 不可能的

by a whale on a rainy and foggy night is an excellent example of caution." "Certainly," replied Stubb, "I've sent out fishing boats to hunt a whale in much worse storms." "Mr. Flask," I said, turning to the short Third Mate who was standing close by, "you have a lot of experience in whaling, and I do not. Is it some kind of unwritten law in whale hunting that a man has to row into the jaws of a wild beast?" "Yes, that's the law!" said Flask.

I now had all the proof I needed to confirm my opinion of what I had to do next. Considering that rowing in heavy rain and horribly windy storms and then capsizing in the sea were normal in whale hunting; considering that I had to row as fast as my arms would permit me into the jaws of a deadly whale; considering that I was doing this because a man who was known as cautious ordered me to do it and, finally, considering the objective of my job was to touch a white whale, there was only one thing to do: write my will and testament. "Queequeg," I said, "come with me, you shall be my lawyer and the executor of my will." It may seem strange that, of all professionals, sailors should spend so much time writing and rewriting their wills, but there is no group of people who like doing this more. After the ceremony of signing the document, I felt much calmer. I had survived my first whale hunt, I had written my will, now I could relax and enjoy my future.

Our journey continued and life on the Pequod went on as always. We sailors worked on the day to day jobs, following orders from the three mates. "Who would have thought a man with only one leg would lead the battle against a whale!" said Stubb to Flask one morning. "If I had only one good leg, you wouldn't see me jumping into a boat. Our Captain does strange things." "I don't think it's so

strange," answered Flask, "He's got both knees, he manages just fine." "I don't know," Stubb replied, "I've never seen him kneel."

Many people who know something about whaling argue that it is never a good idea for the captain of a ship to risk his own life while hunting whales. A captain is too important to the mission to put himself in danger. In Captain Ahab's case, considering he had only one good leg, there should have been no question – he should never get into a small fishing boat to lead the chase against the whale. Certainly the owners of the Pequod would not have permitted it, had they known what Ahab was doing. If the owners of the ship had known exactly what Ahab had done, they would have asked him to resign[1]. Ahab had given himself a boat and five extra sailors, none of whom were known to the shipowners. As time passed, the five strange sailors found their place among the other seamen. But the white-turbaned Fedellah remained a mystery until the end. No one ever understood anything about him. He seemed to come from another world and to have a certain kind of power over Ahab. He wasn't like the other sailors, he was a frightening, mysterious creature.

Days and weeks passed and the Pequod sailed forward, past the Azores, Cape Verde, Rio de la Plata and the Carrol Ground, near St. Helena. We were sailing in these calm waters one moon-lit night and all the waves seemed touched by silver. On that night a silvery jet was seen in the distance - a herd of whales were swimming ahead of us. Fedellah saw them first. By now he had a habit of standing in the masthead every evening to watch for whales. Normally, nobody hunts whales at night, it is too dangerous; not one whaler in a hundred would lower a boat to go after a whale by night. Despite this, Fedellah began shouting, "There she blows! There she blows!"

1. resign: 辭職

from high up on the masthead. We all rushed to the front of the deck trying to see the whale jets blowing in the silvery moonlight. The ship was going fast, but soon we could not see the whales, they were much faster than us.

A few nights later, when we'd almost forgotten what we had seen, the same event happened. We heard the shout, "There she blows! There she blows", but again our ship was too slow to catch up with the whales.

We found ourselves in a very bad storm when we arrived at the Cape of Good Hope. "Cape of Good Hope do they call you?" I asked myself. It should have been named Cape of Torment, like in ancient tales, that's how dangerous it was. The Pequod was tormented by a very rough sea and strong winds. We were condemned to rock furiously back and forth across waves as high as mountains. It felt like the storm would last forever. During all this time Captain Ahab continuously remained on the flooded, dangerous deck, giving us commands with a reserved but tragic expression on his face. At dramatic moments like these, nothing can be done but passively wait until the storm passes. A captain and his seamen become practical fatalists[1] – nothing is in their control, they must depend on Nature. Captain Ahab stayed on deck for hours and hours, with his ivory peg leg in its pivot hole, and one hand holding a sail tightly. He stared straight ahead, the rain and snow almost freezing his eyelashes together. Meanwhile the crew, who had been pushed back from the forward part of the ship by the severe wind and dangerous waves that burst over the deck, stood in a line on the side decks, back towards the stern of the ship. Each man had wrapped[2] a rope around himself and tied it to the rail; it was the only way to make

1. fatalists: 相信宿命的人

2. wrapped: 包起來

sure he wouldn't be thrown from the deck by the exploding water that crashed onto the Pequod. Few or no words were spoken; it seemed like the sailors were made of painted wax[1]. The storm continued, days passed, but the demonic[2] waves wouldn't stop. Captain Ahab resisted; he left the deck for short periods only. Starbuck could never forget how the old man looked, down in his cabin, sitting up straight in his chair in his hat and coat, with rain and melted ice slowly dripping onto the floor around him.

Starbuck could see one of the sea charts on the table beside the Captain. It was unrolled and he saw the currents and tides clearly marked on the paper. Captain Ahab was holding a lamp tightly in his hand, letting it swing back and forth with the force of the waves. Though his back was straight, his head was leaning back and his eyes were closed. He was asleep. "Selfish old man," thought Starbuck. "How can you sleep in this storm? Can you still be dreaming of your revenge?"

1. wax: 蠟　　　　　　　　　　2. demonic: 惡魔似的

FIRST - Gapped Text

1 **The following sentences have been removed from the first two paragraphs of Chapter Five. Choose from sentences 1 – 4 the one which fits each gap. There is one extra sentence you do not need. Do not look back at the text until you have completed this exercise!**

1 "Is it some kind of unwritten law in whale hunting that a man has to row into the jaws of a wild beast?"

2 Well, there is nothing like the danger of whaling to make sailors feel like this.

3 "Can you tell me, Mr. Flask, if Mr. Starbuck has written laws about whaling?"

~~**4**~~ You cannot take what happens around you seriously because if you do, the seriousness of everything might be too difficult to tolerate.

There are certain unusual times in life when what you are doing, the situations you find yourself in, all seem like an enormous joke. ....*4*.... When you are feeling this way, the universe seems surprisingly cheerful; all difficulties and worries, even danger, seem distant and improbable – someone out there is teasing you, nothing bad can possibly happen to you.

(A) .... After the first battle with a whale, I started thinking just that way. When they pulled me out of the water, the last man to be saved from the sea, I lay on the deck, trying to catch my breath. "Queequeg," I asked, "does this sort of thing happen often?" Without much emotion, though soaking wet and breathing hard just like me, he told me that such things did happen while whaling, very often. "Mr. Flask," I asked the Third Mate, "You have a lot of experience in whaling and I do not. **(B)** .... "Yes, that's the law!" said Flask.

Stop & Check

2 **Answer the following questions.**

1 How does the reader know Ishmael has survived a very dangerous accident?

2 Why should the captain of a whaling ship never risk his own life?

3 What would the owners of the Pequod have done if they had known what Ahab did during the whale hunt?

4 In what ways did Fedellah remain a mystery to the other crew members?

5 What was the weather like when the Pequod arrived at the Cape of Good Hope?

6 Why do the captain and the crew become fatalists?

7 What could Starbuck never forget?

8 What does Starbuck think about Captain Ahab at the end of the chapter?

Writing

3 **Do you think Captain Ahab is selfish or foolish? Why / Why not? Support your point of view with examples from the text.**
Is anyone else on the Pequod selfish and/or foolish? Who? Why?

....

....

....

....

....

....

....

....

....

....

Vocabulary – Make and Do

4 **Match each word with the correct definition.**

1 ☐ squid
2 ☐ fathom
3 ☐ tow

a a measure of depth used at sea, about 1.8 meters
b to pull something forward with a rope or chain
c a large sea animal with ten arms around its mouth

Vocabulary – Expressions with Get

5 **Put one of the following expressions with *get* into each sentence. Be careful to use the right tense according to the context.**

> get closer • ~~get a look~~ • get hungry •
> get caught • get back • get angry

Ishmael was able to ..*get a*.. good ..*look*.. at the other whaling ship.

1 The Pequod .... to the ship so the sailors could have a 'gam'.

2 Captain Ahab .... if the 'gam' went on for a long time because he wanted to find Moby Dick.

3 It took a long time to .... to the ship because they had killed the whale a long distance from the Pequod.

4 If a seaman .... in a harpoon rope it is very dangerous.

5 Ishmael did not .... when he saw Stubb eating a whale steak.

Vocabulary – Make and Do

6 **Put these expressions under the correct column. Then complete the sentences using the correct tense of *make* or *do*.**

one's way • progress • a job • ~~one's best~~ • oneself heard • friends • one's duty • a comment • ~~a noise~~

MAKE	DO
a noise	*one's best*

..."*Make no noise*"... said Ahab when they saw the Sperm whale. Ishmael ..._*did his best*_... to ignore the whalers superstitions about the squid.

1 The captain of the whaling ship Albatross tried to .... to the Pequod.

2 The Pequod .... northeast through kilometers of 'Brit', a strange sea plant.

3 It was difficult to .... because there wasn't very much wind.

4 Ishmael .... with Queequeg very quickly after they met.

5 The sailors ....; they always followed Captain Ahab's order.

6 Ishmael was surprised when Queequeg .... about an angry god.

Chapter Six

Life at Sea

One day, as we were sailing southeast of the Cape of Good Hope, a tall sail appeared ahead of us in the distance. As we got closer, I was able to get a very good look at the ship since I was up high in the front masthead. I could see a ship ahead of us, the Albatross, which was almost completely white; it had been at sea for four years so its paint had faded in the sun and all of its metal parts had become rusty from too much sea water and salt. The sailors looked just as worn down[1] as the ship.

"Hello, ship ahoy, have you seen the white whale?" someone shouted out from the Pequod. The captain of the Albatross raised his trumpet[2] to his mouth to answer, but at that very same moment, it somehow fell out of his hand and into the sea. He tried to make himself heard without it, but in the strong wind it wasn't possible to hear anything he said. Unfortunately the two ships were sailing quickly in opposite directions.

What do whaling ships usually do when they meet another whaler in decent weather? They have what is known as a "gam". Gams are friendly social occasions between the captains and crews of two ships. The men exchange letters, books and learn about each other's success at hunting whales.

1. **worn down:** 精疲力竭   2. **trumpet:** 喇叭 ▶SYN◀ megaphone

That day, the weather wasn't very good at all so we had no choice but to watch the Albatross disappear on the horizon. Even if the weather had been good, it's likely that Captain Ahab would not have stopped for any social occasion, judging by how he behaved at other times when the Pequod met ships. The only thing he cared about was news of Moby Dick; he didn't want to waste time, not even five minutes, talking to other captains or sailors.

We headed northeast and sailed into waters that were covered with a strange yellow substance called Brit. Brit is the plant which a certain breed of whales, the Right whale, eats. It is one of many kinds of food found in the sea. The Right whales we saw that day were relaxed; they had no Sperm whales to fear (men are not the only animals who are afraid of great white sperm whales) and could swim slowly through the watery fields of Brit, their mouths open to take in as much of their plant food as possible. The whales were like giant mowers, cutting huge paths of pure seawater behind them; they left no trace of Brit in the water. The sea holds many unseen secrets, whereas on land, everything is visible and clear. Historically, man has always been afraid of the sea: it is an everlasting, unknown world; it's a 'terra incognita'[1], and, we must remember, two thirds of our earth is covered by water. Mankind comes from the sea, but we cannot return to it!

As we made our way northeast through kilometers of Brit in the water, the Pequod was tranquil in the light breeze. One blue morning when the sea was very still, the harpooneer Daggoo saw a huge white mass floating in the distance. It slowly sank under the surface and could be seen no more. Was this Moby Dick? thought Daggoo. The animal rose up, its white mass clearly visible

1. terra incognita: 未發現的領域

under the sun. "There it is, there it is, the white whale!" shouted Daggoo. Hearing this, the seamen rushed to the sides of the ship. Standing in the sun without his hat, Ahab stood at the front of the ship, staring at the sea. Immediately, he gave orders to lower the harpoon boats and it was only a matter of minutes before they were in the water. Ahab's boat was in front, but we were all rowing quickly, trying to reach the whale. We didn't know if it was Moby Dick or not, but the animal we saw was certainly one of the most beautiful secrets you can find in the great seas. The cream-colored mass, with innumerable long arms radiating from its center, lay on its back, floating in the water, in harmony with the world. Slowly, effortlessly, it disappeared down into the sea. Starbuck stared at where the creature had sunk and said, "I almost wish I'd seen Moby Dick, and had a battle with him, than to see you, you horrible white ghost!" "What was it, sir?" asked Flask. "The great live squid. You know, people say few whaling ships have ever seen it - and returned to tell their story," replied Starbuck. Captain Ahab said nothing, just turned his boat around and sailed back to the ship. We all followed, silently.

Whatever superstition whalers have in regard to seeing this squid, you can be sure the fact that it's rarely seen gives the story great power. It is seen so rarely that almost every whaler in the world is convinced it's the largest, strangest animal in the entire ocean. Legend wants us to believe that the sperm whale's only food is this particular fish.

If Starbuck thought the squid brought bad luck; for Queequeg it brought something different. "If you see that squid, you can be sure you'll soon see a sperm-whale," he told me while he was sharpening[1] his harpoon.

---

1. **sharpening:** 削尖

The next day was extremely humid and still, there wasn't any wind at all. There wasn't much to do on the ship and the Pequod's men could barely resist the urge to sleep in such a quiet sea. The part of the Indian Ocean where we now found ourselves was known for being a bad place to hunt. You didn't see much at all, no dolphins, porpoises or flying fish. It was my turn to stand in the masthead and while I was leaning against the sail, enchanted by the rocking of the waves and the warm weather, I suddenly saw bubbles of air coming up from the water, not forty fathoms[1] away. Before I could shout out, a gigantic Sperm whale began to rise to the surface. As if touched by a magician's wand, the sleepy ship and all the sleepers on it woke up at the same time and shouted "There she blows! There she blows!".

"Lower the boats, lower the boats!" cried Ahab. The sudden shouting of the seamen must have surprised the whale because as the harpoon boats went into the water, it swam away from us. "Quiet men! Make no noise," ordered Ahab. The whale didn't go fast or very far and was actually quite near Second Mate Stubb's boat. As happens in cases like this, the man who is closest to the whale has the honor of hunting it.

Stubb urged his men to begin the attack. "Go on, go on men! Start, start! No hurry, take your time, be careful but go, go!" Stubb shouted. He turned to his harpooneer Tashtego, "Start her Tash, strike, strike! Keep cool, cool, but go, go!" "Woohee, wahee!" cried Tashtego, raising his arm into the air to throw his harpoon. "Keehee, keehee!" yelled Daggoo from his boat. "Ka-la, Ka-la!" shouted Queequeg. And so with shouts and oars flying, the boats moved forward towards the whale. Meanwhile Stubb urged his men on, "Tash, give it to him, now!" Tashtego threw his harpoon. The harpoon hit the whale and

1. **fathoms:** 噚，測水深的單位，大約1.8米

went deep into its body. There is a rope connected to the harpoon, while the other end of the rope hangs loosely. The harpooneer can hold this end, or tie it to the boat. It's called a whale line and is very long and can be very dangerous for the men on the boat if their arm, or leg or body gets caught in it, especially if it is attached to a whale. "Go back, back men, back!" yelled Stubb. "Wet the line, wet the line!" shouted Stubb, to stop the rope from burning Tashtego's hands. Tashtego was standing up, holding the whale line with all his strength in order not to fall into the sea. The boat moved closer to the whale. "Pull it back, pull it back!" Stubb ordered his men to row backwards, fighting the power of the whale. The whale was bleeding and the water around him turned red. The harpoon boat was now close enough to the whale that Stubb could throw his lance[1], hitting the whale directly. The whale slowly stopped moving and finally rolled over. "He's dead, Mr. Stubb," Daggoo said. "Yes he is," said Stubb, staring at the enormous corpse[2] he had made.

Stubb's hunt had ended at a distance far away from the Pequod. That meant we had to work together to tow the whale all the way back to the ship. The gigantic body was very heavy and it took a few hours for us to get back. It was almost dark by the time we returned to the ship, but the lights were on and we saw Ahab waiting. The captain had been active during the hunt but now that it was over and we had our trophy, he seemed to have lost interest. It was as if the sight of a white whale only reminded him that Moby Dick was still out there, still had to be hunted. If Ahab seemed disappointed, Mr. Stubb was thrilled with his conquest[3]. Stubb greatly enjoyed his victory. "Ok men, tie up that whale!" he told us, "I want a whale steak for dinner!" Even though we were exhausted, we had to follow his

1. **lance:** 長矛
2. **corpse:** 屍體 ▶SYN◀ dead body

3. **conquest:** 戰利品

orders. We tied its head to the stern and its tail to the bows so it was attached to the Pequod, half in the water, half out.

Stubb was the only man to dine on whale because sailors don't usually eat whale meat, but he wasn't the only creature to enjoy a whale dinner that evening. Along the side of the ship where we had tied the whale, you could see a lot of sharks, eating as quickly as they could and fighting each other to have more. Stubb was too interested in his own meal to worry about the sharks, he would take care of them later. In fact, after finishing his dinner, Stubb ordered Queequeg and another sailor to begin their attack on the sharks. It was not a pleasant scene, watching the men killing the sharks. Sharks will eat whatever they can and so, while Queequeg harpooned one shark, another would turn and attack its injured brother. "I don't know which god made sharks, a Christian god or a pagan one, but the god who made sharks must be an angry god," said Queequeg.

FIRST – Gapfill

1 Complete this summary of Chapter Six with ONE appropriate word for each gap.

As the Pequod was sailing southeast of Cape Good Hope, another ship appeared in the distance. It was (**1**) .... the Albatross and its captain wanted to stop the Pequod to have a gam. Unfortunately the wind was very strong and it wasn't possible for the captain to make himself heard without his speaking trumpet which had (**2**) .... into the sea. The Pequod continued its journey and saw a yellow colored sea plant called Brit. This plant is (**3**) .... by Right whales, but not by Sperm whales. The crew saw another strange sea creature - the giant squid. Starbuck (**4**) .... the squid brings bad luck, but Queequeg (**5**) .... agree; he thinks the squid will bring a Sperm whale. After Stubb and his men kill a whale, he (**6**) .... a whale steak for dinner. It is unusual for whalers to eat whale, but (**7**) .... for sharks. Queequeg thinks (**8**) .... created sharks must be angry.

Stop & Check

2 Answer the following questions.

1 What did Ishmael notice about the Albatross when he first saw it?
2 What do whaling ships usually do when they meet each other on the sea in good weather?
3 Why doesn't Ahab want to stop and talk to other captains or whalers?
4 What do Right whales eat?
5 Why is it necessary to keep the harpoon rope wet?
6 What does Starbuck think it means to see a giant squid?
7 Who had the 'honor' of hunting the white whale?
8 How long did it take to tow the whale back to the Pequod?
9 What did Stubb order Queequeg and another sailor to do about the sharks?

Vocabulary

3 **Match each word or phrase with the correct definition.**

1 ☐ peel off

2 ☐ epidemic

3 ☐ Shakers

4 ☐ mutiny

5 ☐ threaten

6 ☐ melt

7 ☐ bounce

a to hit a surface and move quickly away, like the movement of a ball

b a refusal to obey the authorities, usually by sailors or military personnel

c to express an intention to punish someone if they do a particular thing

d the rapid spread of a disease to people in the same area

e American religious group who live a simple life and do not have sexual relations

f when a solid substance, usually ice, becomes liquid

g to take the skin off something

4 **Fill in the gapped text from Chapter Seven with the following words. Use your dictionary to help you.**

> ~~because~~ • on • to • in • for • of • from

Sperm whale oil is valuable ...*because*... it's used for so many things. It lights lamps and is fuel (**1**) .... machines. The most precious part (**2**) .... Sperm whale oil is used (**3**) .... make skin cream and candles. This oil, called spermaceti, is the most difficult to extract (**4**) .... the whale. A sperm whale's head has two parts, the case and the junk. Spermaceti oil is only found (**5**) .... the case, and only a very talented harpooneer knows how to open it. Tashtego was our spermaceti specialist (**6**) .... the Pequod.

Listening

5 Listen to the beginning of Chapter Seven and choose the correct answer (A, B, C or D) for each question.

What does everyone know about a whaler's job?
A ☑ When you are a whaler you can never rest.
B ☐ It is difficult.
C ☐ Whalers never work on Sunday.
D ☐ They don't care about anything except whale oil.

1 Where is whale oil found?
A ☐ In the whale's tail.
B ☐ In about one third of the whale's body.
C ☐ In the whale's fins.
D ☐ In the whale's skin.

2 Who is an expert at cutting whales?
A ☐ Ahab
B ☐ Ishmael
C ☐ Starbuck
D ☐ Stubb

3 What is whale blubber?
A ☐ Beef
B ☐ Plastic
C ☐ Fat
D ☐ Skin

4 What does Ishmael think when he sees the whale's head completely cut from its body?
A ☐ He thinks it's horrible.
B ☐ He thinks it's pretty.
C ☐ He thinks it looks like an orange.
D ☐ He thinks it looks frightening.

Chapter Seven

Getting the Whale Oil

▶ 7　The next morning was Sunday, the day of rest. Everyone knows a whaler can never rest, not even on Sunday. We had to start the difficult job of cutting the whale. The sharks had eaten quite a lot of our prize, but they weren't interested in the only thing we wanted – the precious whale oil. We had sailed for thousands of miles to reach this goal and at last we had arrived at the purpose of our voyage.

Whale oil is found in the head of the whale so that was the first part of the body we cut. It wasn't an easy job because a whale's head is very large – it is about one third of the entire body. Fortunately, Stubb was an expert at cutting whales, and he enjoyed his work very much. It was my first time at a whale cutting so I had a lot to learn. I saw Starbuck and Stubb holding their long lances; they were suspended in air, hanging from ropes on each side of the whale. They each began cutting a hole on opposite sides of the body, near the whale's fins[1]. This is done to make room for a large hook[2] which they then put into each hole. When the hooks are inserted into the sides of the head, it can then be pulled up, cut at the spinal cord. At that point, it is ready to be separated completely from the body.

Before I continue with the story, I should probably explain something about the whale's skin. The most important question

1. fins: 魚鰭　　　　　　　　2. hook: 鈎

is, exactly what and where is the skin of a whale? You might have already heard of the term 'whale blubber'. Blubber is something like beef in consistency, but it's tougher and you can stretch it. It seems very strange to describe skin in this way, but there can be no other name for the substance that is the outside layer of an animal's body. Technically, blubber is whale fat, but I think it can be described as something similar to skin.

It isn't necessarily easy to separate the whale's blubber from its body, but here's what you do: you cut a hole in the side of the whale and put a hook attached to a rope inside it. Then you cut a deep line along the side of the whale, and pull the rope so the whale starts rolling in the sea. As the whale rolls, the blubber will start coming off its body. If you can imagine the rind of an orange when it peels off, you can imagine what you have to do to get whale blubber. It comes off the whale in large pieces which are called 'blanket pieces' because the whale is literally wrapped in the blanket of its skin.

After the blubber is peeled from the whale, its body is lifted out of the water. It isn't a pretty sight I must say. The whale's head is cut completely from the body and suspended over the ship's forward deck. The rest of its body is left in the sea. The head was so heavy, hanging from the ropes, that the Pequod leaned forward under its weight.

▶ 8   It was 12 noon on that Sunday when, with the whale's head hanging over the deck, the men took a short break to have their lunch. A few moments passed and Captain Ahab came up from his cabin. He looked at the whale's head, paused, and then picked up Stubb's long lance which was still there on the deck. Ahab used it to strike the whale's head while he stared at what remained of the animal. He

began whispering, "Speak to me, you enormous head, tell me your secrets. Of all divers, you have dived the deepest. Who and what have you seen? You have known the mysteries of the sea!"

"There's a sail, there's a sail!" cried a happy voice from up in the masthead. "Ah, that's a relief. That lively shout would cheer up any man!" said Ahab, "Where's the ship?" "Not far, not far at all!" was the reply. "Very good my man, I feel better and better!" shouted Ahab.

While Captain Ahab had been talking to the whale, the whaling ship Jeraboam sailed into sight. An epidemic of some type had broken out on the ship which meant we couldn't have one of our social gams because we didn't want the epidemic to spread to our ship. However, the captain of the Jeraboam had an important message for Captain Ahab; he wanted to speak to Ahab very much. Captain Mayhew had a problem with one of his sailors, Gabriel, and wanted him to leave his ship. According to Mayhew, Gabriel, who belonged to the religious sect known as the Shakers, was a bad influence on the other sailors. Gabriel believed himself to be a prophet, and earlier during their voyage had ordered Captain Mayhew to get off his own ship! He had almost created a mutiny[1] against the captain. A few days later, when they came to the next port, Captain Mayhew tried to force Gabriel off the Jeraboam. The crew believed in Gabriel and threatened to quit if he was dismissed. Captain Mayhew was forced to let Gabriel stay on board.

While the two ships were getting close enough for the captains to talk more easily, Stubb recognized one of Mayhew's rowers. "That's Gabriel, he sees the future. He sees evil in the world," said Stubb. He had heard Gabriel talking at a gam with another boat. He knew Gabriel had a reputation as a very strange person. Stubb thought he represented evil.

1. mutiny: 叛亂

As Captain Mayhew's boat got closer to the Pequod, Ahab said, "I'm not afraid of your epidemic Captain, come on board." But at that moment, Gabriel stood up and began to shout, "Think of the fever, think of the sickness. Beware the horrible plague!" "Gabriel! Be quiet, be quiet, Gabriel!" shouted Captain Mayhew. Unfortunately, a big wave hit Mayhew's boat and his words couldn't be heard. "Have you seen Moby Dick?" shouted Ahab. "Curse[1] the giant fish! Beware of his tail!" screamed Gabriel. Again, a sudden wave hit Mayhew's boat, making it impossible to communicate. At that point, Mayhew's men made their own decision to turn around and go back to their ship. It wasn't clear what Gabriel was trying to tell us. Were his words a warning? Was it better to stop hunting Moby Dick?

After this strange interruption, we sailors on the Pequod went back to the work of getting the sperm whale's oil.

Now that the blubber had been removed from the whale's head, one of the harpooneers used a very sharp knife called a boarding sword to cut into the blubber three times. He told us to stand back, out of his way. He cut the blubber into two large pieces so we could start the process of melting it. This was the precious liquid, or sperm oil, that we would put in barrels and sell back home in Nantucket.

Sperm whale oil is valuable because it's used for many things. It lights lamps and is fuel for machines. The most precious part of sperm whale oil is used to make skin cream and candles. This oil, called spermaceti, is the most difficult to extract from the whale. A sperm whale's head has two parts, the *case* and the *junk*. Spermaceti oil is only found in the *case*, and only a very talented harpooneer knows how to open it. Tashtego was our spermaceti specialist on the Pequod. We all watched as he carefully tied a heavy rope around his

---

1. **curse:** 詛咒

waist and then maneuvered[1] his way into the top of the whale's head while hanging from the long rope. You must remember the head is gigantic – a man can easily sit inside the head of a whale. Tashtego used a large bucket which he lowered into the hole he'd cut in the whale *case* and filled it with spermaceti. He was balanced inside the head, using one hand to lower the bucket and the other to hold on to the rope. He was filling and refilling the bucket so quickly that he suddenly lost his balance. Since his hands were slippery with oil he couldn't hold on very well. To our horror, he fell into the sea. A few seconds passed and we couldn't see him at all. "Man overboard, man in the water!" shouted Daggoo. Almost at the same instant, the ropes holding the whale's head broke and it fell into the sea, on top of Tashtego! Released from the weight of the whale's head, the boat bounced back and away from where the head had fallen. Now poor Tashtego was in serious trouble, possibly sinking down to the very bottom of the sea. Suddenly a naked figure holding a sword was seen diving into the water. Next we heard a splash and realized Queequeg had gone into the water to save Tashtego. Minute after minute passed and we saw and heard nothing. Then Daggoo cried, "There, there!" A hand and then an arm came out of the blue water. "It's both of them, both!" cried Daggoo with a happy shout. We could see Queequeg fighting the water with one arm and holding Tashtego with the other. We got them onto the deck quickly, but it took Tashtego some time to come to, and Queequeg didn't look at all well either.

How did Queequeg manage to save Tashtego? While he was under the water, diving after the head, he managed to cut holes in it with his sword. He was like a doctor as he reached into the whale's head and 'delivered' Tashtego from inside, just like a baby. Thanks

1. **maneuvered:** 小心地移動

to Queequeg's great skill, Tashtego was reborn. There are few men as brave as Queequeg, and few ships luckier than the Pequod. After this episode, we had all our men and gallons and gallons of precious sperm whale oil.

FIRST - Comprehension Questions

1 **Choose the correct option.**

What is the goal of the Pequod's journey, according to Ishmael?

A ☐ Killing Moby Dick.

B ☑ Getting sperm whale oil.

C ☐ Sailing around the world as fast as possible.

D ☐ Staying alive.

1 Why does Captain Ahab speak to the whale's head?

A ☐ He has gone crazy.

B ☐ He is very superstitious.

C ☐ He is obsessed with finding Moby Dick.

D ☐ He believes whales can talk.

2 Why can't the Pequod and the Jeraboam have a 'gam'?

A ☐ Captain Mayhew doesn't want to speak to Ahab.

B ☐ Ahab doesn't want to stop his ship.

C ☐ There is an epidemic on the Jeraboam and the whalers on the Pequod don't want to get ill.

D ☐ Gabriel is a dangerous man.

3 What does Gabriel tell Captain Ahab?

A ☐ He is sick and has a fever.

B ☐ He wants to go fishing.

C ☐ Moby Dick is near.

D ☐ He should stay away from Moby Dick because the whale is evil.

4 Why did Tashtego fall into the sea?

A ☐ He was working very quickly, lost his balance and couldn't hold on.

B ☐ A large wave hit him.

C ☐ The rope around his waist broke.

D ☐ He was pushed by another seaman.

5 How did Queequeg manage to save Tashtego?

A ☐ He swam as quickly as possible from the Pequod.

B ☐ He used his harpoon rope.

C ☐ He used a bucket.

D ☐ He cut a hole in the whale's head and pulled Tashtego through it.

Stop & Check

2 **Which character or characters in Chapter Seven...**

...was an expert at cutting whales? .... *Stubb*

1 ...was talking to the whale's head? ....

2 ... was the captain of the Jeraboam? ....

3 ...believed himself to be a religious prophet? ....

4 ...recognized Gabriel? ....

5 ...fell into the sea? ....

6 ...rescued Tashtego? ....

Vocabulary

3 **Match each word with the correct definition.**

1 ☐ float

2 ☐ wound

3 ☐ gangrene

4 ☐ malicious

5 ☐ vice

6 ☐ casks

7 ☐ leak

8 ☐ hammock

a to hold on to something to stay above water and not sink

b very large wooden containers

c intended to harm caused by hatred

d the decay and death of a part of the body because there is no blood

e a hole or gap where liquid or gas can come out accidentally

f an injury, often made by a knife

g a type of hanging bed made from material or net

h a device which holds things very tightly between two parts

Matching

4 **Sentences 1-4 are from Chapter Eight. Match each one with a sentence A-E that has a similar meaning.**

    [D] Do you see this?

1 ☐ All of a sudden I was blinded by some black foam.

2 ☐ Yes, but what we should leave alone is often what we want most.

3 ☐ The only real owner on a ship is its captain.

4 ☐ You must beware of yourself.

A Suddenly I couldn't see anything.

B You must obey anything the captain says on a ship.

C You are putting yourself into a dangerous situation.

D Can't you see what happened from this?

E Sometimes, what we want very much will hurt us.

Word Categories

5 **Put these words from Chapter Eight into one of the following categories. Some of the words may be used in more than one category.**

> rifle • hump • arm • back • tail • oars • leg • nails •
> casks • harpoon • mouth • bones • lance • head

Human body	Whale body	Weapons and tools for whale hunting and whaling ships
nails		nails, rifle

77

Chapter Eight

The carpenter and the Coffin

1   "Ahoy Ship, Ship Ahoy!" yelled Captain Ahab as, again, we saw a ship with a British flag coming towards the Pequod in the water. Ahab was standing at the front of the deck, holding his trumpet in one hand and the ship's rail in the other. The captain of the other ship could easily see Ahab's ivory peg leg as he sat in the bow of his ship, relaxing. He was very darkly tanned, well-dressed and seemed to be good-natured. He was wearing a bright blue jacket, one sleeve of which was empty; there was no arm inside.

"Have you seen the white whale?" shouted Ahab. "Do you see this?" answered the captain, holding up the white arm that was made of ivory from a sperm whale.

"Lower my boat, lower my boat!" Ahab ordered his men. It took no time at all for him to be lowered into the sea, helped into his whaling boat and rowed over to the British ship. In his excitement, Ahab had forgotten how difficult it was to get from a whaling boat into a whaling ship – if you only have one leg that is. He suddenly stopped, embarrassed and angry with frustration. Just as suddenly, the other captain understood the problem and quickly lowered the blubber hook that whalers use to peel whale blubber from the animal. Ahab was able to sit in this enormous hook, and was pulled

up and onto the deck of the one-armed captain's ship. With his ivory arm pointing forward in welcome, the captain walked towards Ahab, who, stepping firmly on his ivory leg, met him on the deck. "Yes, yes, let us shake bones together! An arm and a leg, an arm and a leg!" said Ahab. "Where did you see the white whale? How long ago?" he asked.

"I saw the white whale over there," said the Englishman, pointing east with his ivory arm. "There, that's where I saw him, last season." "And he took your arm off, didn't he?" asked Ahab. "Yes, he was the cause of this, he was. And he took your leg, didn't he?" responded the captain. "Tell me your story, tell me about it," Captain Ahab insisted.

2   "It was the first experience like that I'd ever had. I knew nothing about the white whale at that time. One day we started hunting a group of 4 or 5 whales and my boat got attached to one of them by a harpoon. The whale went around in big circles until, at a certain point, a second, absolutely enormous great white, with a milky-white head and hump, came up out of the water."

"It was him, it was him!" Ahab cried. "He had harpoons in his fin," said the captain. "It was Moby Dick it was! Those were my harpoons!" shouted Ahab. "Let me finish, let me finish, sir," said the Captain. "Well, this old grandfather whale started attacking my harpoon line; he kept trying to cut it with his teeth!" "That's an old trick, I know him," Ahab interrupted.

"I don't know what it was exactly," said the captain "but somehow our line got caught in his teeth and we were pulled directly onto his hump! He was so large and such a great prize that I decided to capture him. I was sure the line would come loose and we could kill him. I jumped into the boat closest to him, and raised my harpoon. All of a sudden I was blinded by some kind of black foam made

by the whale's tail in the water! It was directly in front of us, like a wall of watery marble. He crashed his tail in the water, then raised it again. We couldn't attack him, we had to escape, but it was too late. The waves he had created with his tail flooded my boat and I went flying – straight towards his mouth. His jaw closed and I felt a strange sensation on my shoulder – when I looked at it, I saw a huge cut in my arm, from my hand to my shoulder. There was a lot of blood, I had never seen so much blood. I lay on my back and floated, but if you want to know the rest of the story, you'll have to talk to that gentleman over there because I don't remember anything else," said the English captain. "Captain," he said to Ahab, "this is the ship's doctor, Dr. Bunger. Bunger my friend, the captain."

3   The doctor had been listening quietly to his captain's story. He had a round, sober face and was well dressed, like most gentlemen of his social class. "It was a horrible wound, shocking," said Dr. Bunger. "Captain Boomer took my advice and steered old Sammy…" "Samuel Enderby is the name of our ship," added Captain Boomer. "The captain steered our Sammy to quiet waters so we could take care of his arm. The wound got worse and worse and I feared the worst, gangrene[1]. Captain Boomer's arm was completely black at this point and there was only one thing to do; I had to cut it off," said the doctor.

"What happened to the white whale?" asked Ahab, who had listened impatiently to the doctor's story. "Oh," replied the one-armed captain, "after that we didn't see him for a long time. In fact, I didn't even know it was him until much later, when we heard other whalers talking about him.

4   "Did you ever get close to him again?" asked Ahab. "Twice." "But you couldn't get close enough?" asked Ahab. "I didn't want to get

---

1. gangrene: 壞疽

closer, he already had one of my arms, isn't that enough?" answered the English captain.

At that point Dr. Bunger interrupted the captains. "Whales aren't malicious. They're animals; they attack out of instinct - they don't plan on taking arms or legs." "Yes, Dr. Bunger, no more white whales for me, I hunted him once and that satisfied me. He would be a great prize and he's got a lot of oil in him, but he's best left alone, don't you think Captain?" said Captain Boomer, as he looked down at Ahab's ivory leg.

"Yes, but what we should leave alone is often what we want the most," Ahab replied. "How long since you saw him last? What direction was he going in?" asked Ahab. "Are you crazy man?" said the doctor. "Tell me, tell me!" shouted Ahab, "where was he headed?" "Good Lord, what's the matter? Are you crazy?" asked Captain Boomer. "He was headed east, sir, east."

5   Ahab was unhappy. He left the Samuel Enderby so quickly that he hurt himself and his ivory leg. When he jumped from the ship into his whaling boat he cracked the top part of the ivory. Ahab needed to trust his leg completely, so he did the most practical thing to repair it – he called the ship's carpenter. When the man appeared before Ahab on the deck, he asked him to make him a new leg and told his mates to give the carpenter all the tools and parts necessary. Then Ahab told the carpenter he wanted his new leg finished by that night.

This man was not an ordinary carpenter, he was much more. Most whaler ship carpenters are able to do many jobs, but the Pequod carpenter was truly exceptional. He worked well not just with wooden objects; he was extremely efficient in the numerous mechanical emergencies that happened on a three or four year sea voyage. He

repaired the kitchen stove, repaired the ship's oars, inserted holes in the deck and put new nails in the side planks[1]. If a sailor had a toothache, he could pull out the infected tooth. Another sailor wanted to wear earrings, he pierced their ears. He did most of his work on his vice-bench; a long, rectangular shaped table which had several vices of different shapes. The carpenter was prepared to do whatever was necessary, and he did his work in a calm, impersonal way. He did not seem to work so much by reason or instinct; he worked by a kind of straight forward, unemotional process. If he had ever had a brain, it must have been concentrated in his hands and his fingers.

He followed Captain Ahab's orders and by that evening, had made him a new and perfect ivory peg leg.

6   The next morning everything was back to normal. The sailors were pumping the ship, which was part of their usual routine. Pumping the ship meant cleaning the floor around the casks which hold the oil, to make sure none of the precious sperm whale oil was leaking out. However, that morning there was a problem and Starbuck went to report it to Captain Ahab.

Starbuck found Ahab in his cabin, studying a map of the area which goes from the China Sea to the Pacific Ocean. Ahab was sitting with his new leg leaning on the table, with a serious expression on his face. "Who's there, who's there?" said Ahab when he heard Starbuck's footsteps, without turning around to see who it was. "Go away, go away!" he shouted. "Captain Ahab, listen, it's me, Starbuck, we've got an oil leak, we must stop right away," said the first mate. "What, and lose time, just when we're getting closer to finding Moby Dick!" answered Ahab. "Either we do that Captain or we'll lose more oil than we'll find in a year. What we've come

1. planks: 木板

20,000 miles for is worth saving, sir. It would be horrible to lose so much oil," said Starbuck.

"So it is, if we can find him," Captain Ahab said. "I wasn't speaking about the whale, sir, I was speaking about the oil. The owners back in Nantucket are expecting to see thousands of dollars' worth of oil!" said Starbuck.

"I wasn't speaking about the oil, let it go! Let it leak! We don't have time to fix the leak!" shouted Ahab. "But what will the owners say, sir? They hired us to hunt whales, for their oil!" asked Starbuck. "Who cares about the owners? The only real owner on a ship is its captain! We aren't stopping. Now go, leave me alone!" Ahab shouted.

Ahab was furious. He picked up a rifle and pointed it at Starbuck, "I said go now!"

Starbuck looked angry but not frightened. He remained calm. He got up slowly from his seat and stared at the gun in the captain's hands. "I could tell you to beware Captain, I could tell you to beware of me, but I won't. You must beware of yourself. Beware of yourself." With these words, Starbuck left the cabin.

Ahab walked back and forth in his cabin until he calmed down. He then went up to the deck and found Starbuck. "You're right Starbuck; you're a good man," he said quietly. "Stop the ship, do what is necessary to repair the oil barrels. Stop the leaks!"

7   The men began searching the casks for the leaks. It was obvious after only a short time that the leaks were in casks that had been put under the others, at the bottom of the ship. The seamen had to work very hard, lifting and moving cask after cask until they finally found where the leaks were coming from. Queequeg worked very hard, as usual, and unfortunately began to feel ill. He had a fever and

complained of nausea[1]. He was laying on his hammock when I found him. His face looked sickly, he was almost white under his tattoos and he didn't respond when I asked him how he was feeling. "What's wrong Queequeg?" I asked. He looked weak and very thin. When he finally whispered something to me, it was a very strange request. He wanted the carpenter to make him a coffin! He had seen coffins that looked like canoes when we were in Nantucket. He believed he was going to die and wanted to be left in the sea, in a floating coffin. The carpenter was ordered to make a coffin for Queequeg. He came to take my cannibal friend's measurements. After doing this, the carpenter found the wood and nails necessary to build the coffin and went to his vice-bench. Not long afterwards, the coffin was ready. Queequeg stayed in his hammock with his eyes closed. He asked to have some important things put into his coffin: his harpoon, some biscuits and some water. Now that he was ready to die, a very odd thing happened; he suddenly began to feel better and in a few days was healthy again. He didn't need the coffin any more. He used it instead as a kind of sea-chest, a container for clothes, his wooden idol and any other objects that were important to him. Queequeg was a mysterious person; it seemed no one would ever understand him completely.

1. nausea: 噁心

Stop & Check

1 **Are the statements true (T) or false (F)?**

		T	F
	Captain Boomer lost a leg to Moby Dick.	☐	☑
1	Captain Ahab sometimes forgets he only has one leg.	☐	☐
2	Captain Boomer and Captain Ahab are very similar in character.	☐	☐
3	Captain Boomer wants to continue looking for Moby Dick.	☐	☐
4	The Pequod's carpenter only works with wooden objects.	☐	☐
5	It took the carpenter very little time to make Captain Ahab a new ivory leg.	☐	☐
6	Starbuck is very worried about the oil leaks in the Pequod's casks.	☐	☐
7	Starbuck isn't afraid of Captain Ahab.	☐	☐
8	Queequeg is afraid he's going to die.	☐	☐
9	He wants Ishmael to make him a coffin.	☐	☐
10	No one knows why Queequeg suddenly feels well again.	☐	☐

Summary

2 **Chapter Eight has been divided into 7 sections. From the list below, choose the sentence (A-F) which best summarizes each section (1-7) of the chapter.**

	An expensive problem.	6
A	A mysterious solution.	....
B	Two important people meet.	....
C	A terrifying experience.	....
D	Doctors know best.	....
E	An extraordinary man.	....
F	We don't always make the best choices.	....

Grammar

3 **Complete the following sentences with the Past Perfect or Past Simple of the verbs in brackets.**

The Pequod ...*ran*.. (run) into a terrible storm; some of the crew ..*had*.. never ..*experienced*.. (experience) such bad weather.

1 The day after the storm, the crew .... (clean up) the wood and rope that .... (blow) onto the deck during the storm.

2 Later that day, Ahab realized that the compasses .... (break) by lightning during the storm.

3 Ahab .... (make) a new compass from pieces of steel he .... (find) on the Pequod.

4 Ahab .... (speak) to the captain of the ship Rachel, who said he .... (see) the white whale the day before.

5 Ishmael .... (be) terrified; he .... (not see) such an enormous animal before.

The Language of Prediction

4 **What do you think will happen at the end of the novel? Use these words and expressions to make predictions about what you think will happen to the following characters: Ishmael, Captain Ahab, Queequeg, First Mate Starbuck, Second Mate Stubb, Third Mate Flask and Moby Dick.**

possibly • certainly • maybe • probably • likely • could • will (not) • might (not)

drown • be killed • get home safely • give up hunting • get lost • escape • catch • survive

I think Moby Dick will be killed by another whaling boat.

1 ....

2 ....

3 ....

4 ....

5 ....

6 ....

Chapter Nine

Candles, Compasses and the Final Chase

▶ 9 We had enjoyed beautiful weather for many days, but all good things must end, even in the Pacific Ocean. We were somewhere not far from Japan when the weather turned bad. It wasn't bad weather, it was much worse; it was a huge storm. The wind, rain and lightning tore off the Pequod's sails making it almost impossible for the ship to move in the turbulent water. Starbuck stood on the quarterdeck trying to see, after every flash of lightning, how bad the situation was. "This is bad, very bad," said Second Mate Stubb to Starbuck. The crew was trying to hold down the whaling boats which were swinging back and forth in the violent wind. A huge wave hit the ship and Captain Ahab's boat was completely filled with water. It looked like it would soon fall from the side of the ship. Stubb starting singing a song about the ocean, he was shouting and laughing. "Stop Stubb, stop!" shouted Starbuck. "Let the storm make noise, but be brave, and be quiet!" the first mate cried. "But I'm not a brave man, I never said I was," Stubb answered. "I sing to keep myself happy." At that moment - a moment of total darkness when there wasn't any lightning - a voice was heard. "Who is it?" shouted Starbuck. "Old Thunder!" Ahab replied. The captain was trying to walk along the deck; he couldn't see where he was going except when flashes of

light came from the sky. Suddenly the lightning struck and we could see that each mast was burning. They looked like very tall candles burning in the stormy, black sky. We sailors were shocked, what kind of sign was this? What did it mean? It had to be a very bad omen. "Turn the ship around, we have to turn the ship around!" shouted the crew furiously. "This is a very bad thing, this is all Ahab's fault," said Starbuck. "He's obsessed with the white whale. He doesn't care what happens to the ship, or us!" When the crew saw Ahab, he had a wild, crazy look on his face. "Look men, look at the candles, look closely. They lead the way to the white whale. The flames are beautiful, the fire is greater than I, greater than us all!" Ahab cried.

"The boat sir, your boat!" shouted Starbuck, as Ahab's whaling boat fell into the sea. The captain's harpoon, which had been in the boat, somehow landed on the deck of the Pequod. It was burning! Starbuck grabbed Ahab's arm and said, "The Lord is against you Captain, can you not see that? Our voyage is evil, it is doomed to end badly! Let me turn the ship around now, before it's too late!" shouted Starbuck. "He's crazy, Ahab is crazy!"

The crew heard Starbuck and ran to their places on the deck to start turning the ship in the opposite direction. There were no sails, no way to control the ship. The men were shouting in their panic. Ahab held his burning harpoon high in the air, like a torch. "You have all taken an oath[1], you have promised to hunt the white whale, just as I have done. Any man who quits now, any man who does not follow my orders, will face this harpoon! We will not turn the ship around. We will go forward."

The next morning the weather was better but the waves continued to push the Pequod forward too quickly. The wind was very strong;

1. **oath:** 誓言 ▶SYN◀ promise

the whole world seemed blown by its force. Captain Ahab stood silently on the deck, watching the sea and the waves. "My ship is like a chariot[1] on the sea! I am its master!" he shouted. Suddenly he was quiet, as if he had just thought of something important. He went quickly to the helm[2] and asked, "What direction are we going in?" "East-Southeast, sir," answered the frightened sailor who was steering the ship. "You're lying! Heading east at this time, with the sun over there?" shouted Ahab, pointing to the bright sun high in the sky. At that point, we were all confused. How was it possible that no one had noticed this mistake? Ahab looked at the compasses, his instruments for navigation, and we thought he would collapse with shock. They were broken. Our guiding instruments had been destroyed by the storm! Before the crew could understand the dangerous consequences of this event, Ahab started to laugh. "Oh, I have seen this happen before Mr. Starbuck. You've never heard of this before I imagine," said the Captain. "I've heard about it, but never before has it happened to me," said Starbuck unhappily.

Lightning from the storm that we had luckily survived, had electrified the most important compass on the ship. If one compass is destroyed by lightning in a storm, all the compasses are destroyed.

Captain Ahab looked up at the sky again. He measured the position of the sun and realized the Pequod should be going in the opposite direction. He gave the order to turn the ship around. Starbuck said nothing to the captain, he simply obeyed his order. Stubb and Flask did the same thing. They were all more afraid of the captain than of anything else.

"Men," said Ahab, "the storm destroyed my compass but I can make another one." He held a piece of steel and other tools he had

1. chariot: 馬車　　　　　　　　　　2. helm: 舵

asked for. "I can make a compass that will be as good as any other," exclaimed the captain. If you could have looked into his eyes, you would have seen Ahab's fatal, arrogant pride.

The storm had almost destroyed our ship, but only the crew seemed to understand this. Ahab's obsession with finding Moby Dick was all that mattered to him. Starbuck wondered what would happen if he killed the captain, but he was a good man. Starbuck knew he was incapable of killing another man.

The following day the weather turned beautiful. On the horizon we saw another ship, the Rachel. We were travelling at a good pace because the winds were strong in our sails, but the storm had damaged the ship, it was not the same. We were all on the deck, cleaning away the broken wood and rope that had blown everywhere on the ship. As the Rachel got closer to the Pequod, the wind changed direction and we slowed down. "Bad news, there's bad news coming from that ship," one of our sailors whispered.

As soon as the boat was near enough to the Pequod, we could hear the captain's voice asking the same question he always asked. "Have you seen the white whale?" shouted Ahab. "Yes, yesterday, we saw it yesterday. Have you seen a whale boat?" was the answer. "No, not yet," Ahab cried, with joy. He seemed reborn at the news that Moby Dick wasn't far away. The captain of the Rachel wanted to come on board our ship. Ahab usually didn't like gams because they took time away from our search for the white whale, but this time he was happy to greet the fellow captain. He recognized him as someone he knew from Nantucket. "Captain Gardiner, tell me about the whale!" said Ahab, "Where was he? He's still alive, isn't he?" "Yes he is," said Gardiner. Gardiner could see that Ahab was happy to

learn the white whale had not been killed. He looked at Ahab with a strange expression on his face.

"I'd like to make a proposal, Captain Ahab," said Gardiner. "Why don't we hunt Moby Dick together? We would be stronger if we worked together against him. We sent out three of our fastest whaling boats to hunt him, but only two came back. We don't know what happened to the third boat. My son is on that third boat Captain Ahab, I beg you to help me find him," Gardiner said in a desperate voice. "I'll pay you for your help, you must help me, you must! I would do the same for you if it were your son Captain Ahab. I won't leave this ship until you promise me you'll help me find my son," cried Gardiner.

I hadn't known until that point that Ahab had a family waiting for him back in Nantucket. It was hard to believe a man like him could have people who loved him.

"Enough Captain Gardiner, enough. I will not help you. I am already losing time by talking to you. Moby Dick is close and I must follow him," said Ahab. "Goodbye, good luck and forgive me, but I must go." Ahab turned quickly around, put his head down and returned to his cabin. Captain Gardiner was deeply upset. All he could do was get into his boat and go back to the Rachel. We seamen remained on the deck, shocked by what we had just witnessed. How could Ahab have refused to help Gardiner? Starbuck was amazed by what the captain had done. "Sir, sir, can you not think of your own family? I too have a wife and family. Let's go back to Nantucket, back home. Let's turn the ship around now," Starbuck said. Ahab stared at the sea and answered Starbuck, "I don't know what drives me forward. Maybe it's God, or just my fate. Do I have to hunt the white

whale? Yes, yes I must! It's my fate!" Hearing Ahab, Starbuck knew the truth, his captain was crazy, he was a victim of his own obsession.

It started in the middle of the night under a clear, starry sky. Ahab was on the deck, even though it was late at night because he was sure Moby Dick would appear. "Man the mastheads, man the mastheads!" shouted the captain. "What do you see, do you see him?" he asked the sailor. "Nothing sir, nothing," was the reply. "I'm going up, I'm going up to the masthead!" Ahab cried. "There she blows! There she blows! The gold coin is mine! It was my destiny – only I could see him!" the Captain shouted as loudly as he could.

"Lower the boats, lower the boats," ordered Ahab. "Ishmael, help us lower the boats," Starbuck said to me. Soon all the boats except his were in the water and the men were rowing as fast as they could. Ahab's harpooneer, Fedallah, looked pale but fierce, like an animal on a hunt for another animal. I stared at the water and was terrified by what I saw – the gigantic, pure white hump of the biggest whale I had ever seen. As he rose up in the water we could all see his forehead, his twisted jaw and many broken harpoons stuck in his huge back. Despite his size, he didn't seem to be so dangerous, he seemed to be enjoying himself in the water. He seemed like a gentle, happy animal. Could this be the cruel killer we had heard so much about?

At that point he put his head down and sank under the water, completely out of sight.

A flock of birds called Herons[1] were flying above us. When you see Herons it usually means a whale is about to come to the surface of the water. Suddenly the birds began flying directly at Ahab's boat. "The birds! The birds!" shouted Tashtego. Ahab remained with his eyes fixed on the sea but saw nothing. But then, as he stared down into the

1. herons: 鷺

depths of the sea, he saw a small white spot, no bigger than a mouse. The white spot rose quickly in the water and we could see two rows of enormous teeth – the teeth of the white whale. Ahab managed to turn the boat around, pick up a harpoon and prepare himself for the battle. Moby Dick was quicker however. As he came up, faster and faster, he opened his mouth and, as his huge jaws emerged from the sea, some of his teeth got caught on the boat. He played with the boat, shaking it like a cat with a mouse. Captain Ahab's head was only a few inches from that mouth! Moby Dick pushed the boat up and up – Captain Ahab and all the men in his boat flew up in the air and into the water. Meanwhile, not far away, Starbuck watched what was happening from the Pequod. When he saw the captain fall into the water, he sailed the ship towards the whale, to distract it from the men who were trying desperately to swim away from the gigantic animal. Starbuck got Moby Dick's attention for a few minutes and then, mysteriously, the whale dove under the water and disappeared again.

We didn't see him until the next day. Again, we heard Captain Ahab's voice shouting "There she blows, there she blows!" and we saw Moby Dick in the distance. We lowered the boats and when the seamen got close, I saw them throw their harpoons into the whale with all their strength. Moby Dick fought back, twisting and turning violently in the water. He attacked two boats – Stubb's and Flask's. Their boats turned over and the crews were tossed[1] into the sea. Ahab's boat tried to save the drowning men but Moby Dick attacked his boat and the captain flew into the water. The Pequod managed to rescue the seamen and get some of the broken harpoons they found in the water. Fedellah had disappeared and we saw part of Ahab's peg leg floating in the water. "You haven't broken any bones, have

1. tossed: 亂丟

you sir?" Stubb asked the captain. "I'd fight that whale even if I had broken bones!" shouted Ahab. "No whale, no men, no devils can hurt me, Ahab! Mr. Starbuck, repair the boats, we haven't finished with the white whale!" ordered Ahab.

We worked all night repairing the damaged boats and harpoons. The carpenter made a new peg leg for Ahab; everything was ready by the morning.

The weather was perfect and the sea was calm on the third day of our hunt. We heard nothing from Ahab who was up in the masthead, watching for the whale. Suddenly he shouted, "There she blows!". We could see what looked like a gigantic white iceberg in the distance – the great white was there!

I was so frightened my legs were shaking, but I also felt more excited than ever before. Starbuck looked terrified. Moby Dick was moving dangerously in the water that morning, as if he wanted to tell us to stay away from him. But we had no choice, Ahab forced us to hunt the whale.

"Sir, please, let us turn back, before it's too late!" cried Starbuck. "Lower that boat, now!" Ahab responded. Minutes later we saw a horrible sight. Fedellah's body was tied to Moby Dick – by the rope of his harpoon. Ahab was so shocked he dropped his own harpoon into the sea. "Fedellah, what happened to you?" cried the captain. "I will kill you now, with my hatred!" he shouted, and threw another harpoon at Moby Dick. We watched, horrified, as the rope attached to Ahab's harpoon became caught around the captain's neck as he threw it into Moby Dick. Then, when Moby Dick swam forward, Ahab was pulled out of the boat and disappeared under the water. He was there no more! Captain Ahab was dead.

I watched, paralyzed with fear, as Moby Dick swam straight into the Pequod. He smashed his head into the ship, again and again. It was only a few minutes before the Pequod slowly sank under the surface of the water. Ahab and his ship went down to the bottom of the sea together. The endless waves rolled over and over into the horizon, as they always had.

The story is over, the drama done. Only one person survived. It was I, Ishmael. After the Pequod had disappeared, Queequeg's coffin came up to the surface and I managed to catch it as it floated past. I held on to it for twenty-four hours until I was found by another ship. In the end Queequeg had saved my life, and the captain of the Rachel, who had lost his son, found another young man, me.

Matching

1 **Match the two halves of the sentences.**

|b| We had enjoyed beautiful weather for many days
1 ☐ Starbuck stood on the deck trying to see
2 ☐ They looked like very tall candles
3 ☐ Any man who does not follow my orders
4 ☐ If one compass is destroyed by lightning in a storm,
5 ☐ I won't leave this ship until you
6 ☐ Moby Dick pushed the boat up and up,
7 ☐ As Moby Dick swam forward

a Ahab was pulled out of the boat and under the water.
b but all good things must end.
c throwing Captain Ahab and all the men into the water.
d how bad the situation was.
e will face this harpoon.
f all the compasses are destroyed.
g promise me you'll help me find my son.
h burning in the stormy, black sky.

Comprehension Check

2 **Answer the following questions with information from Chapter Nine. Make sure you write complete sentences.**

1 Where was the Pequod when the weather turned bad?
2 What happened to the masts during the storm?
3 What did Captain Ahab make for the ship?
4 What did Captain Gardiner say about Moby Dick?
5 What was Captain Ahab's answer to Captain Gardiner's request?
6 Who saw Moby Dick the first time and so won the gold coin?
7 Describe how Moby Dick attacked the Pequod.
8 How many days did the hunt for Moby Dick continue?
9 What did Starbuck want to do?
10 Who survived Moby Dick's attack?

Speaking

3 Discuss these questions with a partner or in small groups.

1 How much do we learn about Ishmael in the story? Do you like him? Why / Why not?
2 Do you think Captain Ahab is a tragic hero? Does he have a fatal flaw, like heroes in Shakespearean or Greek tragedies?
3 How important is the idea of prophecy in the novel?
4 Are the lives of the characters determined by fate or by free will?

Writing

4 Go back and read exercise 2 on page 18 again. Do you think Moby Dick is an important character in the novel? What do you think he represents? Write a short essay to explain your point of view.

The Life and Times of Herman Melville

Herman Melville was born on August 19th, 1819 in the city of Manhattan, New York. His father, Allan Melvill was a successful man who became rich by importing foreign merchandise. His mother, Maria Gansewoort Melvill, took care of Herman and his seven siblings. She added the 'e' to Melvill to make it seem more American. Herman's early childhood was happy but his happiness was brief. The family business failed at the end of the 1820s. Herman had to start working when he was only 13 because his father died, possibly from the stress of his failure.

First jobs

Herman's first job was in a bank which he didn't like at all. He finished school while working and at the age of 18 became an elementary school teacher. His next job was as a newspaper reporter. He didn't like that profession either, so when he was 19 he became a merchant sailor. He got a job on a ship that was going to Liverpool, England. He went back to the U.S. a year later. He went to Illinois in search of a job. Once again his lack of success only increased his debts so he returned to the East coast.

The whaling experience and his books

Feeling desperate, he signed up for a whaling voyage on the ship Acushnet. He didn't know how long he would be at sea, but he didn't care, he had to work. The journey took him around the world; around South America, across the Pacific Ocean to the South Seas. Conditions on the ship were bad and Melville was forced to work extremely hard. In the summer of 1842, Melville abandoned the ship after 18 months at sea. Another sailor from the Acushnet went with him to the Marquesas Islands where they were captured by a tribe of cannibals. Melville lived with the native tribesmen for a month. This experience opened Melville's mind to new and different cultures. In fact, the experience became the basis for his first novel, *Typee: A Peep at Polynesian Life* which was published in 1846. The book was a combination of fact and fiction and became his personal bestseller – no other Melville book was as successful during his lifetime.

The Acushnet's crew list, December 1840. Herman Melville's name appears sixth from the bottom

MOBY-DICK;

OR,

THE WHALE.

BY

HERMAN MELVILLE,

AUTHOR OF

"TYPEE," "OMOO," "REDBURN," "MARDI," "WHITE-JACKET."

NEW YORK:
HARPER & BROTHERS, PUBLISHERS.
LONDON: RICHARD BENTLEY.
1851.

His experiences living with native tribes and later, working on a British whaling ship, inspired his greatest novel, *Moby Dick*. Ishmael, the narrator of the story, often makes comments about the differences between cannibals and Christians. Herman Melville was one of the 19th century American authors who questioned established ideas regarding social values and human rights. He was also influenced by Nathaniel Hawthorne, author of *The Scarlet Letter*. They became friends and Melville dedicated *Moby Dick* to Hawthorne.

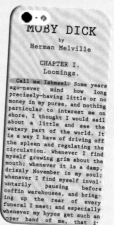

Nowadays Melville is considered one of America's greatest authors but during his lifetime he never achieved real success. Whaling was a dying industry by the 1850s and *Moby Dick* was a failure. Melville died in 1891 a poor, sick man. In the 1920's *Moby Dick* was rediscovered by the literary world and has since become an American classic.

WEBQUEST – The origins of the Tattoo
One of Melville's most important characters in Moby Dick is Queequeg, the cannibal whose skin is covered in tattoos. No one knows for sure where the first tattoos were done but it is probable they originated in Polynesia, according to historical accounts from the journeys of Captain James Cook. Use the Internet to find the answers to the following questions.

1 Which Polynesian islands were visited first?
2 Who first mentioned the word 'tattoo'?
3 Who did Captain James Cook take to Europe?
4 How do Polynesians learn traditional tattoo designs?
5 What was the role of tattoos in Polynesian culture in ancient times?
6 Explain some of the differences in Polynesian tattoo styles.

The Commonwealth of Massachusetts

What to see

Massachusetts is known for important historical events and places. The survival of the Pilgrims in the 1640s, the battle of Concord and Lexington at the beginning of the American Revolution and the birth and death of the American whaling industry are only a few of the amazing events that took place in this state. A visit to Massachusetts is a great way to learn about American history and enjoy the U.S.A. today. You can experience state parks, heritage trails, museums, monuments and battlefields. You can also see where famous American authors such as Ralph Waldo Emerson, Edith Wharton and Henry David Thoreau lived and worked.

Boston

The city of Boston offers a wealth of places to see and things to do. Why not walk along the road made famous by Paul Revere during his midnight ride? It starts in Boston Common and continues, passing 16 sites which were important during the Revolution. If you're interested in witches, stop for a visit at the Salem Witch House, the home of judge Jonathan Corwin. Judge Corwin condemned many women to be burned at the stake because they were believed to be witches.

Your next stop could be Harvard University, where John F. Kennedy received his university degree. President Barack Obama was a professor of Jurisprudence at the same university.

Moby Dick's places

Once you leave the city, why not travel to New Bedford, where you can catch a boat or an airplane to Martha's Vineyard or Nantucket? New Bedford is where the narrator of *Moby Dick*, Ishmael, begins his journey.

Once you arrive in Nantucket, you'll be able to imagine just how courageous the sailors from Melville's time really were. Now the home of whaling museums, beautiful beaches and ports, and a thriving tourist industry, Nantucket was once the whaling capital of the world. As Melville wrote in *Moby Dick*, "Thus have these...Nantucketeers overrun and conquered the watery world..."

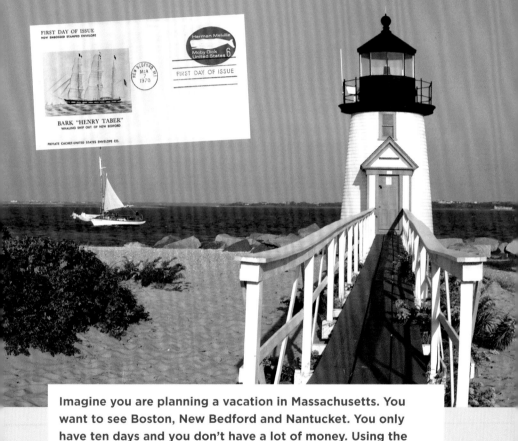

Imagine you are planning a vacation in Massachusetts. You want to see Boston, New Bedford and Nantucket. You only have ten days and you don't have a lot of money. Using the Internet, create your trip. Include the following information:

- your itinerary and transport.
- your accommodation.
- the historic sites and locations you plan to see.

Whaling: Yesterday and Today

The whaling industry

People have been hunting whales for a very long time. 5000 years ago Japanese sailors might have risked their lives just to harpoon these giant fish. Norwegians started whaling 4000 years ago. The Inuit Indians, who hunted in the Arctic Ocean, the Basques in the Atlantic as well as the Japanese in the Pacific, depended on whales to provide many important supplies.

People ate whale meat, skin and blubber for its protein, minerals, vitamins and fats. They used baleen, commonly called 'whalebone', found in the mouths of whales, to make women's corsets, hair combs, toys and carriage whips. The most important product obtained from whales was oil. Whale oil was used to fuel lamps. It was also used to lubricate machinery.

By the mid-19th century, most homes were lit by lamps filled with whale oil. Spermaceti oil, which is only found in Sperm whales, was the most precious. Its unique, rich and waxy texture made candles which burned beautifully, without an excess of smoke. Spermaceti oil was also distilled and used to fuel lamps.

Whaling Ships in New Bedford, MA

The decline of the whaling industry

By the 19th century, whaling was a multi-million dollar business in the U.S.. American whaling ships had developed technological innovations that made them very efficient. These ships had gun-loaded harpoons and travelled on steam. American whaling was based in the northeast with New Bedford, Massachusetts as its center. New Bedford was known as 'the city that lit the world'. The most important whaling expeditions departed from New Bedford or Nantucket. In 1851, when *Moby Dick* was published, whaling had already reached its greatest success. Not long after, the whaling industry began to suffer.

There were two reasons for its slow but steady end. As the 1800s continued, petroleum and kerosene began to replace whale oil as a source of fuel. The petroleum fields in Pennsylvania offered a less expensive and more reliable method for lighting American homes. Another cause for the decline of whaling was overhunting. As early as the 1700s, it had become difficult to find whales anywhere near the Atlantic coast. By the late 1800s, the American whaling industry was in serious decline.

Even without fossil fuels, whaling could not have continued much longer. The world's whale population had been greatly reduced by the early 1900s. In 1946, several countries formed an organization called the International Whaling Commission (IWC). It worked to prevent overhunting of whales. Unfortunately, the IWC wasn't very successful. In 1971, the U.S. listed 8 whale families as endangered species and made whale hunting illegal. Today, whale hunting continues in restricted areas. The debate over the legality of whale hunting also continues; there doesn't seem to be a simple resolution to the question.

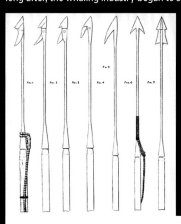

Here are some questions based on the reading.

1   Where and when did early whale hunting happen?
2   What were whales used for?
3   What was the most important product people got from whales?
4   Why was spermaceti oil better than other whale oils?
5   When and why did the whaling industry fail?

Moby Dick Goes to the Movies

More than fifteen films have been inspired by Herman Melville's classic novel. Surprisingly, none of these are considered as truly accurate representations of the book.

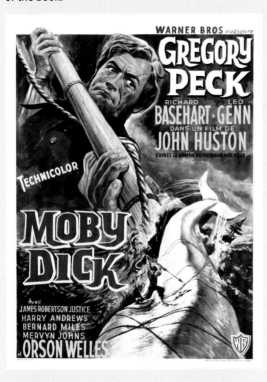

Director
John Huston

The most famous, and perhaps best film, was directed by John Huston in 1956 and starred Gregory Peck as Captain Ahab. The screenplay adapted from the book was written by science fiction writer Ray Bradbury. Richard Baseheart, who acted in Federico Fellini's *La Strada*, played Ishmael, the narrator of the story. John Huston's film is considered great not because it is an exact copy of the storyline, but because the direction, special effects, and acting are brilliant.

Actor Gregory Peck

Gregory Peck said he was embarrassed by his performance as the Pequod's captain in the film. Some critics agreed with Peck; they said an actor who had always played heroes, had always been the good protagonist who everyone loved, could not be an obsessed, half-crazy villain. Most viewers, however, believed Peck's acting was close to perfect and that he was unforgettable in scenes like the Spanish Gold coin or when he and Starbuck argue furiously on the deck. Peck was also in another version of Moby Dick; one made for television in 1998, starring the British actor Patrick Stewart. Peck played the role of Father Mapple in that film with great success.

Director Ron Howard

Ron Howard has directed a film for the BBC called *In the Heart of the Sea* (2015), starring Chris Hemsworth, which is based on the story of the whaling ship Essex. The whaler Essex was destroyed in 1820 by an enormous Sperm whale. As a young man in 1840, during his journey on the Acushnet, Melville met another young sailor named Henry Chase. Chase's father had been the First Mate on the Essex. Henry gave Melville a copy of his father's book, "*Narrative of the Most Extraordinary and Distressing Shipwreck of the Whale-Ship Essex of Nantucket; Which was attacked and finally destroyed by a Large Spermaceti-Whale in the Pacific Ocean*". Chase's story made a strong impact on Melville, and later was the inspiration for his novel.

Writing task

When we go to the cinema or sit in our living rooms watching a film, we probably do not spend much time thinking about the people who made the movie. Actors, directors and all the people who are involved in film-making work very hard to create interesting, enjoyable and good quality entertainment. Look up some information on the internet about the role of film actors and directors. Then, answer this question:

Which would you rather be, an actor or director?
Write an essay of about 150 words. Be sure to include the reasons for your opinion and to divide the essay into paragraphs, including an introduction, main paragraphs and a conclusion.

Choose A, B, or C to complete the sentences about *Moby Dick*.

Ishmael meets Queequeg for the first time
A ☐ on the Pequod. **B** ☑ in an inn. **C** ☐ while looking for a whaling ship.

1 In his prophecy, Elijah says that the Pequod will
A ☐ sink at sea. **B** ☐ never capture Moby Dick. **C** ☐ make a lot of money with whale oil.

2 Captain Ahab wants to hunt Moby Dick
A ☐ to make a new leg out of its bones. **B** ☐ for its whale oil. **C** ☐ for revenge.

3 For many whalers and seamen, Moby Dick was like a
A ☐ symbol. **B** ☐ legend. **C** ☐ hero.

4 During his first whale hunt, Ishmael
A ☐ felt sick. **B** ☐ got separated from the rest of the crew. **C** ☐ ended up in the sea.

5 Near the Cape of Good Hope, the Pequod encountered
A ☐ good sailing conditions. **B** ☐ very bad weather. **C** ☐ a large group of sperm whales.

6 Stubb caught the white whale in the
A ☐ Pacific Ocean. **B** ☐ Atlantic Ocean. **C** ☐ Indian Ocean.

7 During the collection of the spermaceti oil, ... fell into the sea.
A ☐ Ahab **B** ☐ Queequeg **C** ☐ Tashtego

8 The similarity between Boomer and Ahab was that they both
A ☐ had a false limb. **B** ☐ were obsessed by Moby Dick. **C** ☐ were good-natured.

9 For Ishmael, Queequeg was not an easy person
A ☐ to get along with. **B** ☐ to understand. **C** ☐ to share a meal with.

10 Captain Ahab was killed by
A ☐ his own whale line around his neck. **B** ☐ Moby Dick's jaws. **C** ☐ a carelessly thrown harpoon.

SYLLABUS 語法重點和學習主題

Verbs:
Present Perfect Simple and Continuous
Past Perfect Simple and Continuous
Participle phrases
A variety of phrasal verbs
Complex passive forms
Modal verbs – all types
Reporting verbs: explain, insist, reply, shout, answer, cry out, yell

Types of Clause:
Third conditional
Mixed conditionals
Defining and non-defining relative clauses

Other:
Connectives: although, though, even though, despite, in spite of, however
Time sequence
Discourse markers
Inversion

///

Moby Dick

pages 6-7

1 **People:** sad, anxious, cheerful, curious, blue, disappointed, afraid, astonished
   Places: sad, wild, curious
   Weather: damp, rainy, wild

2 **ships/the sea:** deck, masthead, waves, seasick, drown, mast, seawater, hull, stern, sink, crow's nest, rope, sail, bow
   whales/whaling: harpoon, harpooneer, hunt, oil, hump, spout

3 Personal answers

4 1 j, 2 e, 3 g, 4 f, 5 c, 6 d, 7 i, 8 b, 9 h, 10 a

pages 16-17

1 1 Ishmael, 2 Nantucket Island, 3 He decides to leave because he has very little money and nothing to do. He feels sad and travelling makes him feel better.
   4 Queequeg, a harpooneer from New Zealand is the cannibal.
   5 At first Ismael is afraid of Queequeg, but then he realises he has no reason to fear him and he feels a new friendship is about to start.

2 1 intentions, 2 **i**mpersonal, 3 mysterious, 4 hidden, 5 sailing, 6 unhappiness, 7 romantic, 8 logical

3 1 choice, 2 chose, 3 chosen, 4 chose, 5 chosen, 6 choice, 7 chosen

4 1 information, 2 luggage, 3 tours, 4 some, 5 some

5 1 d, 2 c, 3 b, 4 a

pages 25-26-27

1 1 F, 2 F, 3 T, 4 T, 5 T, 6 F, 7 DS, 8 T, 9 F, 10 F, 11 F, 12 F

2 Personal answers

3 1 in, 2 we, 3 explains/says, 4 pay, 5 When, 6 join, 7 who, 8 when/as soon as

4 1 d, 2 e, 3 f, 4 a, 5 b, 6 c

5 1 - 6 - 3 - 2 - 7 - 4 - 5

6 1 D, 2 A, 3 C, 4 C, 5 B

pages 35-36-37

1 1 appearance, 2 bone, 3 quarterdeck, 4 rocking movement, 5 impressed, 6 spoke, 7 gestures, 8 unhappy

2 Personal answers

3 1 had made it from, 2 used to walk, 3 It is difficult, 4 such a surprising, 5 accused Ahab of being, 6 were both obsessed about

4 1 h, 2 e, 3 d, 4 f, 5 g, 6 i, 7 c, 8 b, 9 a

5 1 sleeping, 2 attacking, 3 doing, 4 going, 5 watching

pages 45-46-47

1 1 They are faster, bigger, more ferocious and fearless than other whales.
   2 Moby Dick was larger in size, he had a strange snow-white forehead and a tall hump shaped like a pyramid. The rest of his body was lined and spotted with a strange, whitish colour. He also had an injured lowered jaw.

3 Captain Ahab wants revenge because Mody Dick had attacked him and bitten off his leg. Mody Dick represents all of Ahab's anger and frustration and by killing him, Ahab believes he will find spiritual peace and tranquility.

4 Starbuck hunted white whales so he could sell their oil.

5 Fedellah was Captain Ahab's personal harpooneer.

6 The weather was foggy, misty and it had started to rain.

7 The crew of Starbuck's fishing boat couldn't see the Pequod. They were being rocked by the waves when suddenly they heard the Pequod coming towards them. To avoid being hit, the crew all jumped into the water and the Pequod crashed into Starbuck's boat. Fortunately, one by one the crew were pulled out of the water and back onto the Pequod.

2 **1** b, **2** d, **3** e, **4** c, **5** a

3 **1** condemned, **2** kneel, **3** capsizing, **4** torment, **5** teasing, **6** jet, **7** soaking wet, **8** argue, **9** will and testament, **10** joke

4 **1** take – seriously, **2** take a break, **3** catch on, **4** take sides, **5** catch hold of

5 Personal answer

6 Personal answer

pages 54-57

1 A2, B1

2 **1** Ishmael recounts how there is nothing like the dangers of whaling. He decides to write a will and testament.

2 A captain should never risk his own life because he is too important to the mission to put himself in danger.

3 The owners wouldn't have permitted it and they would have made Ahab resign.

4 Fedellah remained a mystery because no one understood anything about him.

5 The weather was very bad, stormy and windy.

7 They become fatalists because they cannot control the weather conditions.

8 He thinks that Captain Ahab is selfish and consumed with his idea of revenge.

3 Personal answer

4 **1** c, **2** a, **3** b

5 **1** got closer, **2** got angry, **3** get back, **4** gets caught, **5** get hungry

6 **make:** one's way, progress, oneself heard, friends, a comment
do: a job, one's duty
1 make himself heard, **2** made its way, **3** make progress, **4** made friends, **5** did their duty, **6** made a comment

pages 65-66-67

1 **1** called, **2** fallen, **3** eaten, **4** said/thought, **5** didn't/doesn't, **6** eats/ate/has/had, **7** not **8** who/whoever

2 **1** He noticed that it was almost completely white as the sun had faded the paint.

2 They have what is known as a 'gam' - a friendly social exchange between the captains and crews of the two ships. They exchange letters, books and learn about each other's success at whale hunting.

3 Ahab didn't want to stop and talk to other captains or whalers because he didn't want to waste time. He only cared about news of Moby Dick.

4 Right whales eat Brit - a type of plant.

5 To stop the rope from burning your hands.

6 Starbuck thought seeing the giant squid brought bad luck.

7 Stubb had the honor because he was the closest to the whale.

8 It took a few hours to tow the whale back to the Pequod.

9 He ordered them to begin their attack on the sharks.

3 **1** g, **2** d, **3** e, **4** b, **5** c, **6** f, **7** a

4 **1** for, **2** of, **3** to, **4** from, **5** in, **6** on

5 **1** B, **2** D, **3** D, **4** A

pages 75-76-77

1 1 C, **2** C, **3** D, **4** A, **5** D

2 1 Ahab, **2** Mayhew, **3** Gabriel, **4** Stubb, **5** Tashtego, **6** Queequeg

3 1 a, **2** f, **3** d, **4** c, **5** h, **6** b, **7** e, **8** g

4 1 A, **2** E, **3** B, **4** C,

5 **Human body:** arm, back, leg, mouth, bones, head

Whale body: back, mouth, bones, head, hump, tail

Weapons and Tools for whales hunting and whaling ships: oars, casks, harpoon, lance

pages 86-87

1 1 T, **2** F, **3** F, **4** F, **5** T, **6** T, **7** T, **8** T, **9** F, **10** T

2 **A** 7, **B** 1, **C** 2, **D** 3, **E** 5, **F** 4

3 1 cleaned up, had blown, **2** had been broken, **3** made, had found, **4** spoke, had seen, **5** was, had not seen/had never seen

4 Personal answers

pages 98-99

1 1 d, **2** h, **3** e, **4** f, **5** g, **6** c, **7** a

2 **1** The Pequod was somewhere not far from Japan when the weather turned bad.

2 During the storm the masts were burning.

3 Captain Ahab made a new compass for the ship.

4 Captain Gardiner said they had seen Moby Dick the day before. He said the Moby Dick was still alive and he wanted to hunt the whale together with Ahab.

5 Captain Ahab refused Captain Gardiner's request. Ahab didn't want to help Gardiner.

6 Captain Ahab saw Moby Dick the first time and so won the gold coin.

7 Moby Dick attacked the Pequod in an almost playlike manner, like a cat with a mouse.

8 The hunt lasted three days.

9 Starbuck wanted to turn back and give up the hunt.

10 Only Ishmael survived Moby Dick's attack.

3 Personal answers

4 Personal answers

page 100-101

Internet: personal answers

page 102-103

Internet: personal answers

pages 104-105

1 It happened 5000 years ago in Japan and 4000 years ago in Norway.

2 For eating; for making women's corsets, hair combs, toys, and carriage whips; for lubricating machinery; and for fueling lamps.

3 Whale oil.

4 Its unique, rich, waxy texture made candles which burned beautifully without an excess of smoke.

5 1800s, because whale oil was replaced by fossil fuels, and people prevented overhunting of whales.

page 108

1 A, **2** C, **3** B, **4** C, **5** B, **6** C, **7** C, **8** A, **9** B, **10** A

Read for Pleasure: *Moby Dick* 白鯨記

作　　者：Herman Melville
改　　寫：Sara Weiss
繪　　畫：Arianna Vairo
照　　片：ELI Archive, Wikimedia Commons
責任編輯：傅薇
封面設計：楊愛文
出　　版：商務印書館（香港）有限公司
　　　　　香港筲箕灣耀興道3號東滙廣場8樓
　　　　　http://www.commercialpress.com.hk
發　　行：香港聯合書刊物流有限公司
　　　　　香港新界大埔汀麗路36號中華商務印刷大廈3字樓
印　　刷：中華商務彩色印刷有限公司
　　　　　香港新界人埔汀麗路 36 號中華商務印刷大廈 14 字樓
版　　次：2016年7月第 1 版第 1 次印刷
　　　　　© 2016商務印書館（香港）有限公司
　　　　　ISBN 978 962 07 0485 7
　　　　　Printed in Hong Kong
　　　　　版權所有　不得翻印